Train to He

Alexei Sayle is a stand-up comedian, a writer and an actor. His TV appearances include *OTT*, *Whoops Apocalypse*, *The Young Ones*, *Arena*, *Comic Roots* and his award-winning series *Alexei Sayle's Stuff*. His films include *Didn't You Kill My Brother?* and *'Itch*. He has appeared as an actor in many plays and films, including *The Tempest* and *Selling Hitler* and published two other books: *Geoffrey and the Tube Train and the Fat Comedian* and *Great Bus Journeys of the World*.

AN ALEXEI SAYLE MYSTERY

Alexei Sayle
Train to Hell

with additional material by David Stafford

Mandarin

TRAIN TO HELL

First published in 1984 by Methuen London
Reprinted 1984 and 1987
This new edition published by Mandarin Paperbacks in 1991
Michelin House, 81 Fulham Road, London SW3 6RB

Mandarin is an imprint of the Octopus Publishing Group,
a division of Reed International Books Limited

Text and Illustrations Copyright © 1984 Alexei Sayle
The author has asserted his moral rights

A CIP catalogue for this title
is available from the British Library
ISBN 0 7493 0801 X

Printed and bound in Great Britain
by Cox & Wyman Ltd, Reading

The illustrations in this book are by
Alexei Sayle, with the exception of
the pictures from the sleeve of
'Albania Albania' on page 81: the illustration
is by Graham Humphrey, design by Rob O'Connor,
reproduced by kind permission of
Island Records Ltd.

The photograph of Alexei Sayle on
the cover is by Mike Prior and on the
frontispiece is by Derek Ridgers

Contents

Train to Hell

CHAPTER ONE

Archie Sits
on Something Solid

I paid the taxi driver the exact fare. I did not give him a tip, but instead handed him a card which read:

> I DO NOT GIVE TIPS!
> I FIGHT FOR A DECENT WAGE FOR <u>ALL</u> MEMBERS OF THE WORKING CLASSES! LONG LIVE THE PROLETARIAN STRUGGLE!
>
> _____
>
> PUBLISHED BY THE ASSOCIATION OF MARXIST HACKNEY AND LICENCED CAB USERS.

The taxi driver smiled broadly and handed me a card which read:

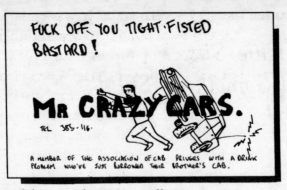

FUCK OFF. YOU TIGHT·FISTED BASTARD !

Mr CRAZY CARS.

TEL 385·116.

A MEMBER OF THE ASSOCIATION OF CAB DRIVERS WITH A DRINK PROBLEM WHO'VE JUST BORROWED THEIR BROTHER'S CAB.

I waved him a cheery goodbye.

I turned and stared for a few moments at the station. Its design was full of solid virtues. It had been created by high-minded northern Victorian railway architects as a lofty cathedral to the spirit of the railway age, the celluloid collar and the pork pie.

But if the station was full of solid virtues, the modern development around it was full of flash notions. This 'precinct' had been designed by bright ex-grammar school boys whose only reading matter in their formative years had been *The Eagle*. They had made concrete the future predicted by the illustrators of Dan Dare and the Mekon, a world where by 1983 all chaps would spend their summer vac on the moon and go to school by helicopter. The precinct burnt down every few years.

I fought my way through the litter and kicked my way past the children vandalising the Photo-Me booths. I located my platform, showed my very special ticket to the very special ticket collector and boarded the very special train. It was eight in the morning, the train was not due to depart until nine-thirty, so I was one of the first on board. Unfortunately I was not the very first. When planning this journey I had taken special care to book a double-berthed sleeping compartment all to myself by buying two tickets (I shout certain things about the Pope in my sleep and it can cause offence and embarrassment) so I was well pissed off to find a pasty-faced teenager sitting bolt upright on one of my two bunks. Life is a minefield for the committed Marxist. I was immediately faced with one of those dilemmas which confront those who try and live their life right and ethical i.e. – should I eject the youth on the grounds that I needed sole use of the compartment, just in case I happened, in my solitude, to think up a totally new strategy for the annihilation of monopoly capitalism? Or should I let an obviously needy proletarian fellow-traveller enjoy a little bit of luxury even if he hadn't paid good hard-earned fucking money for it? In the end I decided to let him be for the present, but if he started telling me about his racing pigeons I'd write an anonymous note to the ticket inspector and have him thrown out. The lad in question said nothing but stared straight ahead. 'Three kopeks short of a rouble,' I thought.

For a while I tried to get him to move by using the English method of standing over him and going 'Hmmp' and 'Grffghnm' but he took no notice. So I gave up and sat on the other bunk and stowed my luggage. Being a seasoned traveller, I always travel light. For this journey my luggage consisted of a tin of macaroni cheese and a forty watt light-bulb. I find these are the most useful items to have with one – when encountering difficulties with foreign customs men, border guards or hotel clerks. All you do is wave the macaroni cheese about, hold the light bulb above your head and shout, 'I am Henry Kissinger from outer space, show me your zip fastenings!' and you usually get what you want, pronto.

On the platform men and women were starting to arrive for our great excursion. They carried about them an air of enormous excitement. I settled back on my bunk and got out the copy of *Cosmopolitan* I'd bought to read on the first bit of the journey. If you're wondering why I was reading a women's mag I'll tell you why – well both of us have got nothing better to do. You see it is awfully difficult to find non-racist, non-sexist reading matter that also has big pictures and not too many long words. The usual magazines sold at station bookstalls and aimed at men are either the up-market wank mag, with titles such as *Executive Sperm* or *Playboy Big Dick*, or they are anally fixated 'special interest' magazines, such as *Model Caravan Lavatory Builder* or *Nut and Bolt Collectors' Monthly*.

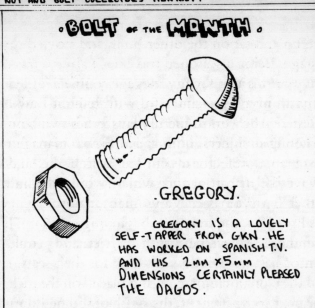

BOLT of the MONTH

.GREGORY.

GREGORY IS A LOVELY SELF-TAPPER FROM GKN. HE HAS WORKED ON SPANISH T.V. AND HIS 2mm × 5mm DIMENSIONS CERTAINLY PLEASED THE DAGOS.

EVAPORATO
NOB. BUT L
THE POODLE
RANGE-RO
THE FACE.
PEACH! MY

THE ARTS

THE "CRAP ON THE RATES" DANCE COMPANY AT THE RIVERSIDE STUDIOS HAMMERSMITH PRESENT A DENSE AND POWERFUL WORK ENTITLED "THE DRAIN" WHICH EXPLORES THE AMBIGUITIES OF HUMAN LOVE. A THEME SUGGESTED BY TWO DANCERS DRESSED ONLY IN FAIRY LIQUID BOTTLES ENDLESSLY RUBBING EACH OTHER WITH MARMITE.

IN AN OTHERWISE SATISFACTORY WORK. I WAS SOMEWHAT UPSET BY THE TOTAL ABSENCE OF EITHER NUTS OR BOLTS. I ALSO DID NOT SEE A SINGLE NAIL OR EVEN A SCREW. THE ONLY HIGHLIGHT WAS THE APPEARANCE OF SOME INTERESTING POP-RIVETS IN ACT THREE.

So give me women's magazines every time. I settled back with my *Cosmo* and read with interest how I could stencil flowers round my lavatory bowl; how two young designers, both called Pippa, managed to shag up a perfectly decent fish warehouse; and how I could fill in a quiz which would tell me whether I was an assertive woman or not.

As I read on, the train was beginning to fill up. I was in the last coach, nearest the barrier, and people streamed past my window heading for their seats. I heard the clunk of luggage being placed on the rack in the next compartment, the swish of sliding doors and the clatter of feet. Every now and then I studied my fellow passenger – after all, people are my business and I consider myself a pretty good judge of character. To me, the youth opposite looked as if he were the sort of person who was always stuffing shredded paper up his nose and pretending to be a turkey. You know the type, don't you? They come round to your house and spit bits of radio-active grit onto the carpet and they're always shouting about how their dad was a dolphin and how their trousers light up at night and they always keep a bit of liver in their pockets and when their conversation flags they whip it out and shout, 'Who wants to see my budgie?' Oh yes, I know their sort, matey, aahh yes, hiding in lampposts and measuring their genitals with bits of string and whispering about the state of my underpants and and, and, erh, erm I, I, I . . . I've come over all queer. Excuse me, I'll just get some fresh air. . . .

Ah that's better!

I was feeling a bit flushed just then and I had to be careful unless I wanted the red mist to ascend again, so I looked out the window for a bit.

It was not quite time for our train to move off, although it was now packed solid. We stood at our own segregated platform. All around our train the dirty and neglected little commuter trains dragged in their loads of early morning office workers, off to another day of 'You Don't Have To Be Crazy To Work Here But It Helps'. As they fled to their jobs they tried not to look at our train, but time and again their eyes slid back towards us and there was fear in their eyes. For our train was of that type which is abhorred by all those straights who ride the rails, our train was that crazed rogue elephant of the tracks, our train was –

A FOOTBALL SPECIAL!

But, you ask yourself, why is Alexei aboard this train? He who had always condemned football as a distraction for the working class, diverting them from their natural inclination towards Marxist revolution and the dictatorship of the proletariat, on a Saturday afternoon. Well, it started like this.

My life has always been tangled around the railway lines. In fact, I was actually born on a train. My father was a railway guard and in the fifties the wages were very poor for that job. After working a forty-eight hour shift my father would often come home tired and weary with only a bag of balloons and a pencil. The only advantage of the job was that all railway workers and their families were entitled to free rail travel anywhere on the trains of Europe. Thus, when my parents knew that I was on the way they realised they could no longer pay the rent on their rose-covered cottage in the village of Toxteth. After much thought they hit upon the idea of us living rent-free on the trains of Europe. They were not the first to come up with this solution to poverty among rail-workers. It is easy to spot somebody who has lived for many years on a train – they can never use a toilet unless it is moving.

Also for me, living on a train, education was a bit of a problem, as I was never in one school for more than fifteen minutes.

At first we travelled mainly in Britain and, as a child, I got to know many of the secret communities that, hidden from the ordinary traveller, live inside railway stations. For instance, at Kings Cross station in London, there is a community of Scotsmen who, having staggered off the Glasgow to London train several years ago, full of McEwans Export and Kestrel (the types of poultry served on trains in those days were much more exotic) have never got further than the Tay Bridge Disaster Railbar where they bumped into a friend of their brother's and got pissed all over again. Many of these unfortunate people live behind the destination boards and haven't seen the light of day for years. Outside pub opening hours they eke out a meagre existence working for British Rail, hiding the luggage trolleys, putting chewing gum on the floor and concealing themselves inside the works of Photo-Me booths, where they make surreal amendments to the passport photos.

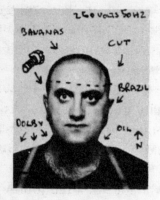

When I was five or six years old our family started travelling, and therefore living, abroad. In the fifties the railway network was much greater and direct connections to the continent were much more frequent. For instance, eight trains a day left Birkenhead (Hamilton Square) direct non-stopping to Tehran (Taramasalata Junction). My knowledge of the international railway system is therefore enormous, and when I won the 'Win Your Chance To Write A Best-Selling Book' competition that I got off the back of a tin of paint (a joint Dulux-Methuen promotion) I felt fate was telling me to write a rail travel book, one of those journals-of-an-international-rail-journey jobbies. But what journey was it to be? All the really exciting trips had been done – by people who had much bigger advances from their publishers than myself. Round the world on a train? Boston to Patagonia? Trans-Siberian? Or, most frightening of all, Leeds to Bradford? They'd all been done. What I needed was a train journey with a really good gimmick. As it turned out I was to get a bigger gimmick than I had bargained for, but I would not find that out until much later.

For a while I gave up the idea of a rail journey. Maybe, I thought, I should just embark on one of those solo round-the-world jobs. I could call the book *Self Obsessed Nob-Head's Travels*. But motor-bikes have been done and if you are going to make a marathon journey and write a best-selling book about it, you need your own unique form of transport that nobody's written about before.

There is a spot where, by tradition, all round-the-world trips start – it is the town southernmost in the world, Tierra del Fuego, Chile. Every five minutes, day and night, some ego-maniac sets off from there. Off round the world, on a bike, on a pogo stick, in a typewriter, with half a pound of Kendal Mint Cake in one pocket and a contract from Methuen in the other.

But solo round-the-world trips are by definition very lonely. After talking to various solo voyagers I realised that the only reason people like Sir Francis Chichester go round the world solo is that they are such twats that nobody will go with them.

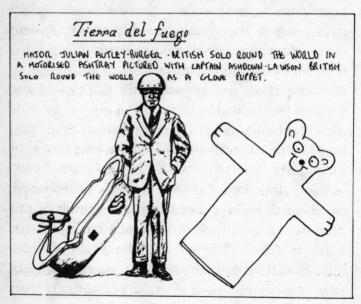

Tierra del fuego

MAJOR JULIAN AUTLEY-BURGER - BRITISH SOLO ROUND THE WORLD IN A MOTORISED ASHTRAY PICTURED WITH CAPTAIN ASHDOWN-LAWSON BRITISH SOLO ROUND THE WORLD AS A GLOVE PUPPET.

No, it had to be a rail journey, that's what I knew about. But what journey? It was in this City, where I am sitting waiting for this train to leave, that I stumbled upon the perfect rail trip.

What a City it was – this jewel of Northern English Industrial Cities! Set on a curving bay, the docks a busy riot of shipping, elegant tree-lined boulevards, small workshops side by side with giant manufactures, gaily coloured trams, a polyglot community living together in harmony – well, that's how it used to be. Now it's like Beirut with job centres.

Showing someone from out of town around, all you can do in the way of sight-seeing is to point to an irregular pile or rubble and say, 'That used to be a really great pub' or 'Over there was a dance hall built as a perfect replica of the Acropolis; it had an oyster bar, a place where airships could tie up and at night it was lit up by primitive laser beams – now it's an irregular patch of mud in the shape of the late General de Gaulle.'

Le Corbusier, the father of modern architecture, once said that a house should be a machine for living in – WHAT A SILLY CUNT! What a fucking nob-headed, shit-faced, bollock-brained, turd-shaped, prick-arsed, wanker-faced cunt! As a result of this silly person and other like-minded persons, the workers in this City we are talking about, were housed in blocks of flats which resembled giant food processors, electric toothbrushes and hair curling tongs. Baffled and dispirited by living two hundred foot up in the air in an offset lathe or a baked bean canner, the workers and their families exist on a diet of Findus French Bread Pizza Style Waffleburgers with seafood-flavoured yoghurt-whip topping. All the supermarkets stock seventy-four different types of biscuits and one hundred and eighty-two different flavours of crisp.

WELL WHAT DO YOU KNOW?

Talking of biscuits, it's a remarkable fact – the number of biscuits named after European re-volutionaries. There's Garibaldi Biscuits, Bourbon Biscuits, Peek Frean's Trotsky Assortment. . . .

In this City of which I write the city council is bent, the police force is bent, the government's bent, the opposition is bent and you still can't get a drink before seven on a Sunday evening.

The train was still not ready to move, although it was now full and armed railway police had blocked off the barrier. The fans rocked backwards and forwards and the train swayed with them. I thought some more about their City. The City had many things it was supposed to be proud of. For instance it is still the ninth largest manufacturer of Those Small Rubber Things That Go Inside Trombones in the whole of Europe.

The people of the City are also supposed to be proud of its possessing the Fourth Best Squodgy Blob of Very Expensive Sculpture Outside a Telephone Exchange in the whole North of

England. And there's probably lots more besides. But in fact there's only one thing the City is really proud of and that's the

FOOTBALL TEAM.

Now this isn't any old football team. This is the classic Bauhaus chair of football teams, the *boeuf en croûte* of football teams, the long red tube with the bit of string on of football teams, the . . . Well, they're very good anyway. Now it's perhaps true that football isn't what it was – and it used to be fucking awful – but this team was special. When that forward line started moving goalwards, opposing defenders would often turn Muslim, change their names and move to Canada rather than face them. Visiting managers tried 4–2–4, 2–4–6, and (01) 888 717 the Guaranteed Goals Company. They tried voodoo, black magic, Marxist dialectics and anti-tank rockets but it was no use. You played them – you lost. And so the City was very proud of their team.

Now it might have been better if the City had been proud of being the birthplace of the Revolution or something like that. . . . Here, comrades, is where they stormed the Telephone Exchange; here is where they shelled Dolcis; there, at that very spot, is the Avenue of the Martyrs of the Fifth Shopping Day Before Christmas; at that very point, comrades, they had a light lunch of reasonably priced rosé wine, brie and crispbread, before charging at the guns of the reactionaries arrayed in front of Chelsea Girl. But since none of this happened, nobody was proud of it.

Quite by chance I was paying a visit to this Northern City in connection with an affair concerning a missing crate of lizards, the unorthodox use of embrocation and several distinguished members of the House of Lords, about which I am sworn not to write further. However, while I was in the City I bought the local paper to read with my lunch and among the usual parochial headlines – 'EARTHQUAKE IN ETHIOPIA – NO LOCAL PEOPLE INVOLVED', 'SUN GOES NOVA IN ALPHA CENTAURI – NO LOCAL PEOPLE INVOLVED' – I read that the famous football team had won their way through to the final of the only tournament they had not yet won – the European Cup, to be played this year in Rome. Furthermore it promised to be a great game, as they were to meet a squad who were said to be the finest flowering of Communist East European football for many years. The two teams had met the year before, but the struggle, although mighty, had only produced an inconclusive draw. Reading on, I learnt that the supporters' club were to take the unusual step of hiring a train which would take five hundred fans direct from the City to Rome, across the railways of Europe. 'That's the train for me!' I thought. 'That's my book!'

The timid office workers were right to look slyly at our train, for it was a very appropriate train for a football special. It looked like the very personification of evil on wheels. It had been built for the 1950 Custom Train Show at Earls Court by that great customiser of trains, Babalou Nesbitt. Starting with a standard British Railways Diesel Loco and five carriages, Babalou and his guys had lowered the roof by a foot which, along with tinted black windows, gave it a real mean street-look. The spec. also included whitewall wheels and two-tone grey paintwork. The original engine had been ripped out and in place of the G.E.C. Diesel, Babalou had utilised twenty-five Vauxhall Cresta engines, complete with chrome exhaust pipes. Unfortunately, the pygmy stylists of the B.R. Department of Aesthetics and Applied Philosophy, obsessed as they were with Design Council-inspired Bang and Olufson-style Swedish Minimalism, could not get their heads around this train and it had lain unused for many years until it was dragged out for this final epic voyage – the greatest football special of all time. Rome and back – a journey which promised hope and rejoicing but (if only we had known it then) would yield a crop of murder, bitterness and despair.

The lights at the end of the platform changed from red to green, the driver let in the twenty-five clutches, put the twenty-five gear sticks into first and we eased away from the platform, out of the station and through the deep cutting. We climbed above ground and ran through the bombed-out inner city. A couple of times kids lobbed bits of concrete at us and somebody opened desultory fire with a .22 rifle but soon we were over the iron bridge which spanned the sluggish brown river and headed south into the bright morning sunshine. Five hundred football fans and me riding the train, the train which, in years to come would be known, in really big letters, as

THE TRAIN TO HELL.

CHAPTER TWO

Wallop!

We were out beyond the city now, clanking southwards through lush countryside. Outside the window the stretches of canal were turning purple, the trees were growing musical notes and giant orange frogs were bouncing up and down, by . . . I've got to stop going round to Kevin's, man, I'm sure that mate of his, Max, puts weird stuff in the yoghurt surprise.

The guy sitting opposite me still hadn't moved a muscle and it was beginning to freak me out, so I decided to take a walk down the coach, in case I started seeing the snakes again.

When I planned my book I made a conscious decision to concentrate on profiling the football fans in the coach I was in (the last coach). After what happened, or rather what will happen, in Rome, I would have no choice, but I wasn't going to know about that until later.

The job of profiling people on the train was made much easier by the fact that this was an official supporters' club excursion, and, in order to keep away unwanted elements, each person who bought a ticket had to fill out a form containing various personal details. The guard of the train kept this dossier. I had figured that with my railway connections I would know him and he would let me sneak a look at his files. And I certainly did know the guard.

I heard the crash and bang of him coming down the corridors before I stepped out to meet him – the legendary Zig-Zag Smith.

Zig-Zag had been a perfectly normal railman until he was attacked by a puma in a tea shop in Richmond, Surrey. The animal, which was owned by a very short man who kept very big animals in his council house, chased Zig-Zag round and round the tea shop and Zig-Zag only avoided its claws by zig-zagging furiously, ricocheting from one side of the room to the other – he finally stunned the animal with a cheese dish. But the damage had been done. From that day Zig-Zag could not walk in a straight line. I saw him now, banging towards me, crashing off the walls of the corridor, occasionally reversing or revolving on the spot, zig-zagging furiously, like the Queen Mary being pursued by U-Boats.

The shock of being attacked by a puma while eating beans on toast in Surrey had also given his conversation a peripatetic quality which matched the randomness of his movements and which he showed as he saw me.

'Alexei! How are you? Never trust an Egyptian with your library books. Barmeeee. How's the family – grape harvest, balloon dance, macintosh?'

Ignoring the swerves of his conversation, I managed to tell him about the best-selling travel book I was writing and could I please have a look at his files. He said sure I could look at his files, then he told me about the latest advances in prefabricated bridge building and I should never wear a top hat in Northern France. Then I followed him as he careered back down the corridor, made several diagonal runs across the large luggage compartment and finally reached his own cabin.

Although we were only a few hours into the journey Zig-Zag, with the experience of a long life on the railroads, had made his berth very cosy.

I settled down with a nice cup of tea and a Belgian bun while Mr Z.Z. Smith, railway guard, gave me the low-down on my fellow passengers on the train which heretofore and wherein subsequently will be referred to as (in big letters)

THE TRAIN TO HELL.

IDEAL COMPARTMENT

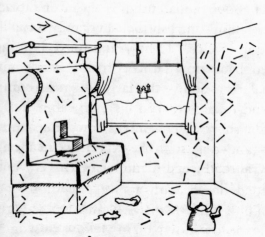

This Month's Feature :-

USING A LIGHTNESS OF TOUCH AND A GENTLEY TEMPERED MODALITY ZIG ZAG SMITH HAS CREATED AN OVERALL GESTALT IN HIS 50's COMPARTMENT. BY USING OBJECTS "JUST SO". AN EMPTY SAUSAGE ROLL WRAPPER HERE AN OLD KETTLE THERE TO CREATE A COMPARTMENT WHICH SAYS "YES I AM". BUT "I ALSO MAY BE".

My notes on the passengers read like this:

'*Our coach*: our coach is divided into the guard's compartment and the luggage van occupying about a third of the carriage, then three sleeper compartments and three seated compartments. The first sleeper compartment is mine. My silent companion, apparently, is called Lance. Unfortunately on his file, under personality is written 'NONE'. The sleeper next to mine has been booked and paid for by a Rabbi Feinstein, but he has not turned up for this outward journey. Again there are no details on him. The third sleeper compartment has been taken over by a film crew from the local B.B.C. station. The only notable person amongst them is Ms Kimberley Clarke. At one time she was a top presenter on *Nationwide* in London in the mid-seventies, but after that programme's swing away from trivia towards serious reportage she was exiled to the north for failing to get an interview with a black pudding that sang old Beatles numbers. In the first seated compartment are two men known as 'Mr Smith' and 'Mr Smith' – can't see why they've got a whole compartment to themselves. When I asked Zig-Zag about these two he went all agitated and muttered, 'Cutpurses! Scallywags! Ask me no more your holiness, Mervyn Peake!' Could be worth investigating. The second seated compartment contains nobody interesting apart from one guy who's called 'The Brain of Football'. Apparently he's a big cheese at these football knowledge quizzes they have and is also a big wheel in the supporters' club. In the final compartment another six football fans – no potential that I can see at the moment. Not much of a haul really. Still, if I don't meet many interesting and exciting characters on the train I can always make a few up.'

The effort of making all these notes exhausted me, so I thanked Zig-Zag for his help then went back to my compartment. Lance, as I now knew he was called, still sat there stiff and silent. If I was going to be stuck with him for the whole journey I thought it was time we got to know each other. The lad was obviously awestruck by my celebrity, but I have a humble cheery conversational tone which I use on simple working-class people. So I chatted to him about football, greyhounds and suchlike until we were circling London. I noticed we were shunted onto the same route as they use for transporting nuclear waste. Although the lad didn't say much, I think I'd put him a little more at ease.

As I slept that night, snug in my compartment, and Lance sat bolt upright on his bunk, our train was loaded onto a ferry, aboard which we crossed the channel. We raced the dawn through Northern France. Anyone who was awake would have seen the station names flash past – Arras, Amiens, Compiègne – names which spoke of an earlier, bloodier conflict – the 1953 U.E.F.A. Cup.

CHAPTER THREE

No Thanks,
I'm A Vegetarian

DATELINE - European Defence Headquarters
Palermo 7.03 am

On one wall of the room a giant map showed all the railway lines of Europe in flashing lines of different colours. Beneath it General Olivetti La Cruizera chomped on a cigar as he stared at his assembled opposite numbers from Switzerland and France.

'Gentlemen, in our time we have supervised the transportation of many dangerous cargoes across the rail network of Europe. Leaky tankers full of the deadliest chemicals; wonky containers choc-à-bloc with nuclear waste; flat-cars loaded with synthetic fabrics in the most abominable taste, destined for the curtains section of Littlewoods catalogue. But this time we face the most deadly, the most contagious cargo ever to travel the rails of our respective countries. You know the cargo of which I speak – five hundred English football supporters, cooped up on one train with no television to keep them quiet. For those of you unfamiliar with

34

dealing with the dangers associated with large numbers of British people outside their home country we have organised this meeting. It is not the violence and damage they wreak which we fear, but it is the terrible contagiousness of their appalling culture. Ask the people of Boulogne and Calais the price they paid for taking British people on their soil on their 'Breakawayafuckadays'. Ten years ago these towns were pleasant French towns, but now!

'I tell you if *just one* football fan leaks off that train and comes into contact with some of our own people the effects would be instant and disastrous. Within days there would be a plague of Britishness sweeping through our countries. Some of the symptoms would be a sudden spread of shapeless Dralon clothes from chainstores; the sudden appearance of shoes that look like camels' snouts; a desire amongst people to "do up" – to paint nice brick houses some awful shade of day-glo orange, to replace sound wooden doors with ones made out of Tupperware – in short a violent outbreak of tastelessness, bad cuisine and anarchy.

'This is the danger we face. We must ensure that not one person gets off that train, except for the match itself, until they are back in their cesspit of a country. Therefore, we have taken the most extreme precautions. This is the whole picture. Along every kilometre of the line there will be armed guards. Starting at our Italian end of the line, some of the finest regiments in NATO will be stationed, poised and ready for trouble, ready to destroy any leakages at source. The line from Rome to Trento will be guarded by the crack "Death's Head Asparagus" division of the Italian Army. These men will be setting a very neat example to other soldiers in their smart Giorgio Armani designed uniforms for the Spring season – you may have heard rumours, but for the first time I can give you details of this entirely new concept in uniform design – just listen to this: leather cloche hats; rabbit fur capes worn over silk blousons with matching silk slim jim ties; culottes in brown cord; and, for the feet, calf-skin slip-ons in claret and blue.'

There was an audible gasp from the assembled soldiers. A ripple of applause went round the room.

'From Trento to the border there will be a division of Carabinieri. They will be armed with the new sub-machine gun designed especially for the Interior Ministry by the Memphis Design Group of Milan. The designer felt that the gun should be an emphatic statement about the nature of guns; it should be the essence of gun-ness. To this end Paolo Vancuzzi has designed a weapon in the palest of pale stained woods from the forests of Northern Germany. The wood is counter-pointed by a metal barrel and stock in the boldest of primary colours. When the gun is fired the bullet in fact goes backwards into the firer thus emphasising the elemental penis-orientation of all weapons technology.

'At the border our Swiss friends will take over with a regiment of their famous motorised pen-knives.

The Modern Swiss Army On Manouvres.

'At the Franco-Swiss border there will be elements of the French Foreign Legion. They will be guarding the train and laying on an exhibition and slide show of venereal diseases from around the world. Between Avignon and the coast France's legendary "Routier" regiment are already guarding the train. This regiment has perhaps the most advanced cuisine in the world. Their Colonel-Chef,

Michel Ricard, has been the pioneer of the most exciting form of cooking this century – the so-called nouvelle "Cuisine Mourir". This, for those of you who don't know – and if you don't know, where've you been – Manchester? . . .' There were chuckles from the tough fighters as General Cruizera continued, 'This "Cuisine Mourir" is the art of serving meat, poultry etc which has been killed in a really interesting and exciting way. For instance, there is "Duck Run Over and Squashed by a Portuguese Tourist Bus on the A5 Near Nantes" and there is the triumphant "Beef Struck by Lightning" and "Chicken Trodden on by Copulating Reindeer".

'Gentlemen, I think with all these weapons at our disposal we can contain these British. Are there any questions?'

General Defarge, Cruizera's French opposite number rose. 'Yes, I have a question. Are the culottes above or below the knee?'

CHAPTER FOUR

Lance's Story

The train clanked its way through Northern France under the solemn gaze of the French army. Lance did not look out of the window, he wasn't interested in abroad. He was only interested in the game. Lance had decided long ago that he wasn't going to miss this particular game. In fact he had never missed a game the team had played – anywhere in the world. He thought of himself as 'Super Fan'. He was saving up all his money so that he could have plastic surgery in order to look more like his idol, the team's striker – Jimmy 'Boy' Wonder.

When Lance was a teenager his parents had tried to thwart his obsession with the team, 'the lads' as he called them. One time 'the lads' had been playing an exhibition match in South America and his dad had said Lance couldn't go and had stationed a regiment of plucky little gurkhas outside his bedroom door to keep an eye on him.

But Lance was a match for Nepalese mercenaries any day of the week, even if they were plucky. In a casual manner Lance told his dad that he was just popping out for a paper and twenty Rothmans. His dad sent a platoon of gurkhas with him but Lance soon threw them off his trail by making random hand gestures and pulling funny faces – a sure way to confuse a gurkha. He then made his way down to the docks where he hid himself in a crate of Those Little Rubber Things That Go Inside Trombones which was bound for Buenos Aires. In the crate he met six of his pals and his sister's boyfriend who, by a funny coincidence, wasn't called Lance.

Lance got to see the match in South America and returned home two months later with an old copy of the *Buenos Aires Chronicle and Advertiser* and twenty cigarillos.

Lance felt that it was a good thing that he was getting away for a bit. The gang that he hung around with down at the baker's shop didn't seem to be much fun any more – and there was another thing. For some reason he kept getting the feeling that somebody had hidden a dog in his room. He knew it was ridiculous but he still thought he needed a break so he was happy to take the train to Rome.

The only problem was food. Like many people in the City, Lance was what they called a 'funny eater'. They were all funny eaters in his family. His sister wouldn't eat vegetables. His younger brother wouldn't eat anything boiled or with onions in it and his dad wouldn't eat anything at all unless Anthony Burgess sat with him to keep him company.

So that he wouldn't have to eat anything foreign, Lance's mum made him a week's supply of cheese and chutney sandwiches and for emergencies he had the address of a shop in Rome that sold Walls' Cornish Pasties. Lance slipped on his Millet's anorak, its pockets bulging with cheese and chutney sandwiches. He said goodbye to his mum, dad, brothers, sister and Anthony Burgess, made his way to the station, boarded the train, saw an empty sleeper and plonked himself down.

In his own way Lance was enjoying the journey, secure in the knowledge that his team were going to thrash the commie desperadoes they were playing against. The only jarring note was this fat bastard in a ripped mohair suit who was hogging Lance's compartment. He said he was writing a book and he was on the telly and he knew Rowan Atkinson as well as any man could – a likely story, the lying cunt. This fat bastard spent the whole time sitting on his bunk sneering and cruelly mocking people, especially those people who had speech defects that they couldn't help. Lance didn't know much about people who were on the telly, but he did know that they were always nice to people, especially those less fortunate than themselves, and they played a lot of golf. (Anyway, despite the fat bastard he enjoyed the outward trip. It was on the way back that the cheese and chutney really hit the fan.)

CHAPTER FIVE

In Which Mr Truelove Comes Unstuck and Ralph Finds More Than He Bargained for in His Suit Pocket

All that day our train poodled south through France. At noon we skirted Paris, then they switched us to the Grande Ligne past Fontainebleau, Laroche, Dijon, Dôle, Mouchard. As evening drew on we crossed the Swiss border at Vallorbe and in the darkness thundered through Lausanne. Across the inky expanse of Lake Geneva was Evian where the expensive water comes from.

Throughout the day I had been mixing with THE PEOPLE. Actually in my coach they weren't really THE PEOPLE, as this was the comfiest of the five carriages, so had been grabbed by anybody who had a bit of power with the supporters' club. While there were no more than fifty people in our carriage, the other four coaches held over a hundred fans each. Whenever somebody from further up the train tried to cross the divide into our coach, one of the elite, who were standing guard, would batter at them with a length of lead piping, shouting 'Reserved! Reserved!'

When we rounded a bend I could see the crush in the other coaches. I could see faces squidged against the window and the odd arm or leg projecting through a ventilator. The wind wafted back to us a stench which grew stronger and stronger as the journey progressed and a low noise — a hum or murmur often whipped away by the wind, but always there — the sound of the working classes on the move.

Anyway, all day I had been mixing with a certain self-serving upper stratum of the people. And I think I can safely say we got on like a supermarket on fire. It's widely acknowledged that I have a free and easy manner with people and these were, after all, my people, assemblers of sprockets, forgers of small rubber bits for trombones, managers of specialist mutton shops.

I am known around town for the high level of my banter, my chit-chat is well up to international standards and my small talk has recently won a Design Council award for contributors to micros-copic conversation. After some initial coolness my sunny disposition and the teeny-weenyness of my chat even began to thaw out Lance — my unwanted compartment-mate. To be frank, it was obvious the lad recognised me from my many appearances in the media and was a bit awestruck to be in my presence. As we chatted, it became clear that my own small level of celebrity and my easy access to show-biz night life fascinated the simple chap. He was all agog to hear about the night Michael Parkinson, Lord Denning and myself spent on a pedalo in the middle of Oxford Circus with three writers from the Reform Club. He was gasping to know whether Norman St John Stevas really keeps a cactus down the front of his trousers and why Billy Joel keeps pieces of liver in the pockets of his safari suit.

The only flaw in our relationship was that Lance seemed to think I'd brought a dog on board with me and had hidden it, somewhere in the compartment. I pointed out to him that that would be a foolish thing to do as the rabies laws are very strict in Britain and the importation of animals is strictly limited – roadies on major American rock tours often encounter great difficulty in getting into the U.K. for this very reason.

While I was getting along with Lance and everybody else in the coach, Zig-Zag was starting to get on my nerves. I couldn't see him but I could hear him. He had taken over the intercom on the train and was running his own radio station which he had named 'Radio Free Football Special'.

One of his most irritating features was that he would give an idiot commentary on every town and village that we passed through. He had also been listening to too much local commercial radio and was trying to imitate their style: 'Hey! (*gurgle chuckle*) it's fantaaastic, rilly, rilly, fantaaastic, (*chuckle hoot*) to have you tuning in (*hoot, chuckle, snort*). Hey, we are just passing through the town of Dijon. That's rilly amaaazing! That's where the mustard comes from. Right? Wow, I can see a shop. Bananas old Bailey, tiptoe Madam? I bet it's a mustard shop! I bet that shop sells over four hundred and sixty kinds of mustard, right? Rilly, rilly, rilly amaaazing! Don't be a fool, Vicar!'

Zig-Zag would also relay bits of news that he'd picked up from the B.B.C. World Service and he played music from an old cassette player. But not only did he provide music and idiot chat, that night Zig-Zag organised a football quiz in the baggage compartment in our coach which was broadcast over the intercom to the entire train.

Each of the five coaches sent a representative to take part. Our representative was of course 'The Brain of Football'. I had not seen him up until then – he was a slight figure with a thin nervous face and long greasy black hair, the most distinctive thing about him was his pac-a-mac. I got the feeling he had a crash-helmet stashed somewhere in his compartment. However, although he was geeky-looking he certainly knew a lot about football. He got every question right in the quiz. Perhaps you'd like to have a go at it yourself.

Question 1: A pitch inspection before the game reveals that while most of the pitch is fine, the goalmouths are deeply rutted and very dangerous. Should you allow the game to be played?

Question 2: Which Football League player has scored against father and son goalkeepers?

Question 3: Name Bratislava Wednesday's goalkeeper.
b) By what name is he better known?
c) Why did he invade Poland?

Question 4: SPOT THE DOG COMPETITION

CAN YOU SPOT THE DOG???

Question 5: Can You Spot The Difference?

Question 6: During a game a player fires a shot. It bounces off a low-flying seagull into goal : who is the Prime Minister of Zimbabwe?

Question 7: ALBANIAN SPOT THE BALL.

Question after question came but the Brain of Football was always there. I accosted him after the quiz as he was leaving the luggage van with the three-piece suite he'd won.

'You certainly know a lot about football,' I said.

'Fuck off you silly cunt,' he replied.

Kimberley Clarke sat squashed in the corner of her compartment and listened with disgust to the football quiz on the intercom. As she had been sent out by the B.B.C. to cover the interesting and exciting things that happened on the trip she should have been filming the football quiz, but it didn't seem likely that they would get any filming done. She was 'in dispute'.

What had happened was that, as per union regulations, there were on the film crew, in addition to the cameraman, assistant cameraman, sound man, and assistant soundman, also two girls for make-up, two boys from wardrobe, three props boys, three lighting men, four O.B. riggers, four grips, two assistant focus-pullers, a set designer, a costume designer and a uniformed commissionaire – all in one compartment.

As soon as the lighting men, known as sparks, had got on the train they realised there was no location catering and had refused to eat foreign food and either wanted Chinese take-aways flown out from England or enormous extra payments 'in readies'. The director refused and started crying. The sparks immediately went on strike and formed a picket line across the door of the compartment. At the same time Wardrobe and Sound had a fight because Sound had moved one of the Roman togas Wardrobe had brought along 'just in case', and that was Wardrobe's job and they were now sulking in a corner along with Make-up – doing each other's hair and bitching about Sound.

Kimberley just kept out of it and kept quiet. She was thinking about her career. She had frankly been on the slide since her great days with *Nationwide* in the seventies. In those days she'd had some great scoops: finding the Cairn Terrier that could play the xylophone; discovering the Renault 5 that could detect fish. Then she'd made one mistake and she'd been transferred to bloody Siberia. The bloody North. What happened there? Bloody strikes, bloody riots, bloody factory closures, bloody sit-ins – not a bloody sign of a skateboarding duck or a psychic rubber plant anywhere.

'But,' she thought with great satisfaction, 'I'm on the way up again.' She hugged the secret to herself but she knew that on this very bloody train there was going to be a story that would put her right back at the top with Angela and Esther. If everything went well in Rome by Christmas she'd have her own show on Breakfast T.V., she'd have her own aerobics record and Cambridge undergraduates would be doing impersonations of her on BBC2. If only it all went well in Rome.

But it didn't.

CHAPTER SIX

Expresso Bongo

The end of Day Two of our journey crept upon us as the Italian border was crossed. The towns of Northern Italy slid past unnoticed as we slept, some of us bolt upright in seats, some of us snug in our jim-jams, dreaming of big pots of Marmite slowly being rubbed into our. . . .?

I had to get up during the night, and as I was walking down the corridor I saw a light coming from the supposedly unoccupied compartment next to mine – the missing Rabbi Feinstein's compartment. Although the blinds were drawn I managed by considerable contortion to see a bit of the inside. What I saw was the woman off the telly – Kimberley Clarke – and the Brain of Football. Kimberley held one of those new lightweight video cameras and she seemed to be instructing the Brain in its use. It looked like a bit of strike-breaking to me, but, as I wandered down to the toilet I thought, 'Why choose the Brain of Football?'

Day Three, eleven a.m., Rome – Roma. A heat haze hung over this, the most exciting and elegant of cities. As we approached the centre I joined four fans who were standing in the door-well of our carriage. They were suitably humbled and impressed by the finest city architecture in the world.

'Look at the state of them fucking buildings.'

'They must be dead old them fucking buildings and nobody's done nothing to dem to make dem nice. No pebble-dash or double-glazing nor nothing.'

'They're dirty, old buildings are. You'd think the council would pull them down and put a nice shopping precinct with lots of parking spaces for one-stop-shopping.'

'Look at dem little shops. They'd give you legionnaire's disease or herpes dem little shops.'

'I'm fucking surprised they haven't put a proper ring road through dem old fucking buildings. Don't the council take bribes here or what?'

At this point our train slid into Rome's central station and the four philosophers shut up instantly, like budgies when their cage is covered.

However, we were not to be allowed off the train. There would be no opportunity for the fans to wander through Rome looking for the best place to buy a really good 1975 Chianti Classico and a kilo of Bel Paese. We would not be allowed off the train until an hour before the game, which was due to kick off at eight that night. We would be marched coachload by coachload to the stadium under armed guard, we would see the match and then we'd be marched back again to our transport.

Contrary to what most people think there is more to being a sports writer than a peculiar haircut, strange clothes and an extra large tie; so I will leave the description of the match to people much better qualified than myself.

Sports Commentators at a charity luncheon

An extract from *My Life is Balls, Memoirs of a Football Manager* by Bob Parsley, As Told to D.H. Lawrence. (Reprinted by kind permission of the Globular Press.)

with a large piece of gâteau.

'It's a tough game though, football – there's no room for emotion. For instance when a player ceases to be useful you have to sell him. Matt Hennessey was a great mate of mine, but when he became old and feeble I sold him to Spurs. Dave Parsnip, he was another great mate of mine and I sold him to some Bedouins.

'Mind you, even my granity old face cracked a bit during that famous match in Rome when we won the European Cup. What a cracking match that was, eh D.H., when with twenty minutes to go, Jimmy Wonder gets into a fight with their striker, what was his name – Ladislav Mplmx – and they both get sent off. What a nightmare! Still we got the winning goal in the last minute, but it was close, damned close. Of course, what happened afterwards was worse. I don't think the club has ever recovered from the . . .'

CHAPTER SEVEN

Whoops–a–daisy!

As I said, I cannot describe the match, largely because I spent the entire time with my face pressed against a pillar with people pissing in my pocket.

After the game we were kept in the ground for an hour. Blimey! No wonder football fans riot. As far as I know the crowds at the National Theatre aren't prodded with sticks, trampled by big horses and searched down their trousers, before and after seeing the latest New Wave Austrian masterpiece on the South Bank.

We armed ourselves with all the usual football chants:

> *Oi! Oi! Oi! Oi!*
> *Keynes is better than Friedman!*
> *Doris Lessing has a greater social conscience than Iris*
>   *Murdoch!*
> *But our team are demonstrably better than most!*

After the crowd had shouted themselves sore, we were released from the ground and were marched, coachload by coachload, back to the station where we waited under the darting eyes of the armed para-military. Our coach was the last coach of the train so we were the last coachload to be allowed to board. The station was now empty except for our group huddled together, surrounded by nervous carabinieri, isolated in a vast expanse of marble floor.

Just as we were about to be moved off there arose a tremendous wailing from behind me. I craned round to see what was happening. A tall rabbi in the whole uniform – black frock coat, cartwheel hat and ringlets, additionally adorned with team rosette and scarf – presumably this was the missing Rabbi Feinstein – was having a tremendous argument with the carabinieri. He was waving his ticket for the train and ululating and calling for the Israeli airforce to come and smite his aggressors. He was making such a fuss that everybody was staring in the direction of the argument. Except me.

You see, one of my hobbies – listed in the *Directory of Marxist Comedians* (Cystitis Press £12.95) along with bottling string and polar exploration – is cycling. In fact at one time I was a professional rider with Team Habitat Sportivo and got into quite a few adventures. (See *Alexei Sayle and the Fucking Big Thing* Flower Press £9.75). But when you are cycling, especially in London, you need tremendous peripheral vision to avoid the hordes of cyclophobic Volvo drivers. You need to develop 'eyes in the back of your arse' as we professional cyclists say, so my angle of vision is something like three hundred degrees and while the Rabbi was performing extracts from *Fiddler on the Roof* at the bemused carabinieri and everybody else, I just happened to notice out of the corner of my eye a figure – a small man completely muffled in team scarf, hat, rosette, etc – slip from behind a pillar on the far side of the station and stealthily creep across the marble towards our little party. Unnoticed by anyone except me this figure slid with incredible athletic grace between the Italian para-military police, and hid himself within our group. At about the same moment the Italians also let the Rabbi through and we were free to move towards the train.

Speed up the video now.

All together in a pack our little legs start to twiddle their way to the barrier. In the centre of the pack a fan in complete team regalia seems to stumble, then slip to the ground, the crowd parts round him, re-forms and moves on a few paces beyond him. Like electricity we all turn at once and see him sprawled on the floor – a knife through his stomach .

Freeze frame.

Go to the toilet.

Bake a cake.

Write a letter to *The Times*.

Start the tape, at normal speed this time.

For several seconds it seems as if the frame is still frozen: nobody breathes, nobody moves, there is silence (quite an achievement in Italy). Then we did not give our names and addresses to the nice Italian Policemen in an orderly fashion. A familiar voice shouted, 'Leg it for the train, lads!' and we turned as one and like a multi-legged animal ran helter-skelter for the safety of the train, bowling over the ticket collectors and diving through the windows and doors like home-bound Calcutta commuters, until all that was left on the station concourse was the Italian Police and a very dead person.

CHAPTER EIGHT

Ending Up

'Well this is a turn for the fucking book and I must say. Here I am, my first entrance, my first page really, and I'm fucking dead, dead, fucking dead. Honestly it's not bloody good enough, it really isn't. I suppose I should introduce myself. Hello, my name's Gavin Coathanger-Smith and as far as I was concerned I was going to have a nice big part in this novel and what happens? I tiptoe across a station, I join a crowd, I go for a little run, and then wallop! I'm lying on a – less than clean, I might say – floor with a bloody great knife sticking out of my stomach. Ooh! It makes me feel quite ill, it does really, seeing it poking out there. Thanks a lot Mr Alexei Fucking Sayle. The music press are right what they say about you. Honestly, I'm well pissed off, I am really. I was promised a lot more than a once-in-a-lifetime opportunity to lie on a floor with a knife in me. I haven't had a chance to use me cockney accent or anything. It all started when my agent, Mr Lewis, rang me and said, "Gavin, are you ready for the big one, mate? Alexei Sayle, you know that fat bastard off the telly, well he's conned Methuen into letting him write this book and their casting people want you for the part of an absolutely crucial character! Now I've had a working lunch with their people and I think I've given them a pretty clear idea of what you're capable of. I think this could be really good for us." (*Us*, God, does he ever listen to himself).

'Anyway, I didn't get wildly over-excited because I've been let down before. I mean Mr Lewis told me, for certain, definite, that I was going to be the Boatman Tai in Salman Rushdie's *Midnight's Children* and he said for sure I would have the job of Golodkin in the book *Gorky Park* by Martin Cruz Smith. But I don't know, somehow when I go for the interview and talk to the authors I somehow don't seem to enthuse enough. They're blagging on about how they're writing the Indian version of *The World According to Garp* (which is a silly fucking book in the first place) and all I'm thinking about is "what terrible cushion covers" or "what a peculiar hair-cut that man's got."

'Of course that slag Andrew Thompson, all he can *do* is enthuse all over authors so what happens? He's Castle, the central character on almost every page in Graham Greene's *The Human Factor* and I'm a dead man on page 57 of Alexei Sayle's fucking *Train to Hell*!

'It really isn't fair. I was much better than Andrew Thompson when we were students together at R.A.F.C. (The Royal Academy of Fictional Characters). I mean I got the award for the Best Minor character in our end of term production of *Lucky Jim*. My bus conductor in the famous last minute dash to the station scene in the later pages was generally acknowledged as brilliant, love. Anyway, when I got the call from Mr Lewis I certainly needed a change. You see, he'd managed to get me a part in *Gorky Park* all right: since the book had come out I'd been lying under a foot of snow with my face cut off, playing one of the bodies. Bloody hell! I suppose that's it – I've been typecast as a fucking dead person. I'm going to spend my entire career lying in mortuaries while other characters prove my previous existences. Bloody great!'

'Anyway I didn't know I was going to be double-crossed at the time, did I? So I thought I'll go along and see the author, the fat turd. So I went along to his council flat that I'm sure he keeps just for interviews in the press. And he's there with his manager (Manager! He needs a handler if you ask me) and this talkative buffoon says how Alexei has got an artistic vision, and Alexei is the authentic voice of disaffected British youth and Alexei can pick his nose with his hands tied behind his back, and laser beams come out of Alexei's arse and, do you know, neither of them offered me a cup of tea and a biscuit. I mean even when you give blood you're supposed to get a cup of tea and a biscuit! So we talked about my character's motivation and all that bollocks, when of course all you really want to know is how many pages am I on and can I use me funny voices. Then the bastard goes and changes his story-line and I'm lying in a pool of me own blood with a fucking knife through me entrails and now there's this wop photographer's just turned up and he thinks he's Helmut Newton or David Bailey or somebody and he's playing funky get-down music and he's taking pictures of me, going "Hold it there". Flash, Click, Wurp. "Yes good! Good! Hold that." Flash, Click, Wurp. "Smashing, lovely, lovely. Yes hold that". Flash, Click, Wurp. Well, what else can I do, you silly Eytie bastard, but hold it — I'm dead.'

CHAPTER NINE

Waka, waka, waka

Chief of Detectives Guido Campagnolo, head of Rome's seventeenth Police District, stared down at the corpse and registered disgust in that typically Italian way by rotating his hips, wiggling one foot, sticking his thumbs in his ears and bending backwards until his head touched the floor. Pasolini, his assistant, registered sympathy in his own gruff Tuscan way by shooting a passer-by.

Guido Campagnolo hated the British and the English in particular. He hated their cruel sense of humour. As soon as the English got abroad they turned into terrible liars. You'd often see a group of English in a bar in Rome all claiming to be John Fowles, author of *The French Lieutenant's Woman*, or in the S.A.S. or hit men for the Arts Council.

And they always gave wicked advice to Italians thinking of visiting Britain – they would tell them that a traditional English greeting was 'Hello I'm a tortoise' or they'd say that the traditional way to address a London policeman was to go up to him and say, 'Hello, I am from Operation Countryman and I claim my five pounds'.

Nobody bought their pathetic cars and shabby clothes any more so they exported hooliganism, unpleasant fashions and situation comedies.

When Guido had been a rookie carabiniero he had had a beat in the old twelfth district – The English Quarter. Of course these English were not tourists, these were the sons of the English upper classes – the really stupid ones, the ones who had once been shipped out to be representatives of now long vanished British companies: Norton Motorcycles, Wolsley Cars Ltd., Associated Cake-Stands Inc., Matchbox Toys. They spoke no Italian, treated all natives as if they were distant cousins of the hamster, and spent all day mutually masturbating each other. Guido was also appalled by their lust for blood sports, fox-hunting, bear baiting, bear dating, cock-fighting.

'Damn these English. Why do they have to come over here to murder each other,' growled Campagnolo in heavily Sicilian accented Italian.

'Too true,' replied Pasolini in heavily Belgian accented Portuguese.

'What?' snarled Campagnolo.

'I said, too true,' said Pasolini in Welsh accented Afrikaans.

'Pasolini,' said Campagnolo, 'If you don't start talking Italian and stop showing off, I'll shoot you – again.'

The English Upper Classes Cock-Fighting

'Sorry Boss,' said a contrite Pasolini.

'O.K. to continue, I was talking about this damned dead Englishman.'

'That's no Englishman,' said a voice in heavily East European accented Italian.

'Pasolini!' shouted Guido, already reaching for his service pistol.

'It wasn't me boss, honest it wasn't,' quacked Pasolini.

Campagnolo stared round. Everything was quiet. Nearby the police artist, Michaelangelo, was sketching a 'scene of crime' drawing on a conveniently vacant ceiling. Then out of the shadows stepped a man, a large man who bore a remarkable resemblance to the late Mr Brezhnev, right down to the clothes – he wore a baggy dark grey double-breasted suit, a large black hairy overcoat and a black homburg hat.

He spoke to Guido: 'It was I who spoke, and what I said is that that dead person is not an English football fan as you might suppose, but that dead person is somebody I recognise and know well. That dead person is in truth the Hammer of the Hungarians, the Bouncer of the Bosnians, the Ruiner of the Roumanians. That dead person is the greatest footballer in the history of my great nation who several hours ago was sent off in the last twenty minutes of the European Cup. That corpse is the corpse of our greatest player, Ladislav Mplmx! I am sorry to drop this bombshell. May I introduce myself? I may be familiar to you, Captain Campagnolo, yes?'

'Well,' said Guido, 'Maybe I've seen your picture during the invasion of Afghanistan. . . .'

'Perhaps,' said Mr Brezhnev, 'but we have met before. I am Captain Slobbo Arsich from my country's People's Bureau of State Security and

65

Library Books★ and in fact we have met before, Captain Campagnolo, at a conference in Geneva on Police Work and the E.E.C. Jam Laws. You may remember my paper on preserves and the one-party state?'

Guido said of course he remembered him, although in truth all the conferences merged into one as did all these East European detectives – they were all the same, trying to buy your jeans in exchange for folk dancing lessons. But then of course Slobbo might have been at the Conference and Guido might have assumed it was Mr Brezhnev, who could tell?

But then thinking about the name, Slobbo Arsich, it suddenly seemed familiar. He had heard plenty of stories, rumours in Police circles (which was as gossip-ridden as any other closed world – which Chief Constables were dating each other, would truncheons be in autumnal shades again this

★An extract from *The Great Terror* by Professor F.M. Kumerasky, (People's Trouser Press KF9-80PZ):

with an enormous piece of gâteau.

In the period of confusion after the glorious revolution of early closing day, one arm of the state, through a series of accidents, became increasingly powerful – this arm of the state was the Library Service. Under its ambitious head, J.R. Allbran, the Library Service became responsible for all counter-insurgency duties. Many people lived in constant dread of a card popping through the door saying "The Noddy Books that you ordered have arrived". Or the appearance of two burly men who would call at midnight to tell you that "There is a fine to pay on your Catherine Cooksons". Or worst of all "Your A.E. Van Vogt is overdue".'

winter? etc.). But he had also heard tales of a great Marxist detective who, for instance, had solved the great Surplus Value Mystery by rigorous application of Marxist dialectics and electrodes to the private parts. A man who was often in conflict with the authorities, in favour one minute and out the next.

'Are you the famous Slobbo Arsich, the Marxist detective?' asked Guido.

'No that's my brother,' said Slobbo. 'It is a curious tradition in my country to give brothers the same name and to attempt to differentiate between them by making one wear an onion tied to his head every second Wednesday. We are a strange and cruel people.'

Guido was too experienced a copper to be taken in by the old 'no, that's my brother' gag, but he let it go. Instead he asked, 'How do you know that this is your countryman Ladislav Mplmx?'

'I am, how you say, associated with the team. As you know, Ladislav was sent off twenty minutes before the end of the game, but he was only noticed to be missing during the post-match folk dance in the bath – about an hour ago. And I came down here on a hunch, I suppose. I knew Ladislav very well. That is most certainly his body. Though why he is dressed in our rivals' regalia I do not know. Still, together I am sure we can find his killer.'

Guido exploded: 'You can just can this "together" shit, Jack! Your telling me he's a countryman of yours puts a whole different complexion on the tin of biscuits.'

The East European pleaded, 'But you must hold the train until investigations can be carried out. The murderer has to be in at the last coach of that train, seeing as its occupants were the only ones present during the murder! That train must be held,' shouted Slobbo.

But Guido was not to be persuaded. He had seen an opportunity for getting those Inglese out of town with no questions asked and he wasn't about to let it slip through his vongole now.

'That's as maybe, but I'm not holding that train for the time it would take to complete an investigation. If they don't go soon there will be no station left – it will be buried under a layer of piss, empty beer cans and stale cheese and chutney sandwiches. These English people are wild animals. So, he is your countryman, I will have him loaded aboard that train and I will also have an international peace-keeping force composed of killers from seventeen different countries placed aboard to guard each door and make sure nobody gets off. The line is already guarded and that train leaves in five minutes, if you want to solve the murder you'd better be on it.'

CHAPTER TEN

Excuse Me, Officer

Slobbo supervised the loading of the corpse of his murdered fellow-countryman onto the luggage van of the last coach. The Italians had put him in a crate marked

DEAD BODY DO NOT BEND

Then Slobbo climbed reluctantly aboard the train. In the corridor, blocking his way, were a pack of the English football supporters. They were certainly a wild-eyed bunch, thought Slobbo, wilder-eyed even than the very wild-eyed Gnarks of distant Tharg province in his home country. These Gnarks are wild-eyed Arghut herders who once a year sweep down into the provincial capital, raid the bookshops and carry off everything they can find by Beryl Bainbridge. Well, these English football supporters were much more wild-eyed than that.

Slobbo thought, maybe we should lighten the mood a little. Maybe he could use some humour from his home country.

'What ho, chaps,' he stammered. 'Here is a humorous story which I read recently in our satirical magazine *Batpshit*. One day a cobbler from Obetz province was working at his work bench fabricating highly fashionable miners' boots in two-tone beige and grey with chisel toes, elasticated sides and two-inch cuban heels for the fashion-conscious bauxite miners of nearby Shomvej town and who should come into the shop but Comrade Vladimir Illyich Lenin, the founding father of the Soviet Union. Comrade Lenin strode up to the cobbler and said to him, "I see you make boots for the proletariat, Comrade Cobbler."

'"That is so," said the cobbler. "Then," said Lenin, "if you make fine boots for the proletariat it must be that the proletarian orientation of the rural petit bourgeois is predicated by and is dependent on the creation of the industrialised bourgeoisie." "They'll be ready Tuesday," said the cobbler.'

Slobbo chuckled to himself: 'That's an example of socialist humour,' he said.

The football fans stared at him in mute anti-pathetic silence. Finally one of the football fans stepped forward and kicked Slobbo in the face: 'That's an example of English humour,' he said.

Well, from that moment on the ice was truly broken, as was Slobbo's nose. Soon a real party spirit prevailed. Slobbo taught them a game from his homeland called 'Nine Men's Shagbot'. In this game one player pretends to be Archduke Ferdinand of Austria. Three players go outside and pretend to be Croatian nationalists and the other five have to guess where the dog is. Then they taught Slobbo a game called 'Give the Man Your Travellers' Cheques'. Then, as the train started with a shudder and a jerk, Slobbo recited some revolutionary poems from his home country.

LOVE POEM

I know my love.
She treads lightly the tightly packed earth
Recently turned over by the plough.
Her hair is the colour of gvon,
Her eyes as bright as newly spun haakskin felt.
She waits for me.
Sucking a T.C.P. throat pastille.

A.V. Dogdurt

WAR

It is night,
Our slit trench is filled with mud,
Our gas capes stink of the morgue,
We huddle in the darkness,
Our lieutenant sings a song from Gnup
    province,

71

A whistle blows,
A shot is fired,
We surrender immediately.

B.V. Lunchun-Voucha

BAWDY TAVERN SONG

Lotte the barmaid,
Oh, Lotte the barmaid.
What an interesting personality she is.
Ha, Ha,
Ho, Ho,
Ha, Ha,
She has read *Keep The Aspidistra Flying*
By George Orwell,
An English writer.
Ha, Ha,
Ho, Ho,
Ha, Ha,
Hee, Hee,
For the price of a glass of quince brandy
She will outline the plot and some of the
     main themes
In an articulate fashion.
Ha, Ha,
Hee, Hoo,
Hu, Hoo,
Tee. Hee.

Trad. (Arr. Neil Diamond)

WISE SAYINGS FROM THE
NORTHERN TERRITORIES
(*collected by Prof. Chas. Ndave, University of Pnuncovac*)

Dead oxen can't breed.
You can't tell the time with a lavender bulb.
Even a beggar can eat a boiled egg.
No man waits on a Wednesday.
Only the hungry starve.

A VERY WISE POEM

Ten shlotti make a kopek,
Twelve months make a year,
But a damaged Kenwood mixer
Will never learn to stir.

'O.K. chaps,' said Slobbo, 'I have to, how you say, cool down the pace now. The very serious situation is this: as you know a person was stabbed and murdered out there on the station concourse. At first it was thought he was one of you lot as he was garbed as you are: hat, scarf, Professor Marten's boots and so on. But no, it turns out this is not English football hooligan reprobate, but football star from my country; greatest star of all time and, to be polite, it seems one of you bastards did him in. My interest in the case is this. I am Slobbo Arsich. What is so funny? Please, do I make joke, break wind, do humorous impression of leading member of Politburo? So, you find my name amusing. So, in my language 'Norman Tebbit' means 'horse who defecates on the door-step of cut-price dentist.' So, no laughter over nomenclature please. I am Slobbo Arsich, Captain in the People's Bureau of Libraries. My duty – to watch over our glorious sportsmen when they are abroad, in case by chance they wander off in some strange city and through lack of orientation and faulty geography find themselves perchance in the American Embassy.

'To prevent this Uncle Slobbo takes everyone on organised outings – what fun and jollity – British National Theatre to see experimental production in cardboard box. Oh, there is nothing footballers like more. Also, our sports persons need special looking after. In Socialist country we are much ahead of you in training processes – six-year-old gymnasts have brain removed and replaced with clockwork mouse, so hop and skip, happy at all times. But, of course, need locking in cupboard at night, which old Slobbo fix. Cycling stars bred from birth, have egg-shaped head, six inch body and four foot long muscular legs, also holes drilled all over for wind resistance – gives urine sample every four minutes. What fun for such a fellow to have Slobbo for a pal. If wanders off, Slobbo gives impromptu kung-fu demonstration.

'So that is me. Regular good guy, all round proper Bobby Charlton. But why me on this train?

Why not Italian police? They say it is not their case. This train is British train, so is little piece of Britain where their writ does not run. Where is the guard of this train. Can you confirm this?'

Zig-Zag stepped forwards. In all his life Slobbo had seen nothing like it. Zig-Zag always punctiliously wore the latest uniform handed out by British Rail's fashion department – he now had on the new Summer Outfit especially designed by Sir Norman Shit. This was a black bomber jacket with chunky orange zip, black S.A.S. style beret and hipster flared trousers. In the eyes of British Rail Executives he looked the epitome of the new age of the train. In the eyes of his passengers he looked like a scruffy cunt. He reminded Slobbo of the lead singer in the dissident rock band Purple Telephone.

Zig-Zag: 'Your information is correct, sir, cocoo, balloon dancers, thank you, general. According to League of Nations Statute, statue, is that youoo, this is a little piece, nay a microcosm, bollocks, Archie Andrews, of Great Britain. All the clocks tell a different time; litter is strewn everywhere; when people say "hello" they mean "goodbye"; class divisions are alive and well thank you; the lights don't work; and anything any figure of authority tells you is a lie.'

Slobbo replied: 'Er, yes, thank you. So it is as the Italians say, this is British soil, or rather this is British rubberised formica that we stand on. The Italians want nothing to do with it, so the corpse has been brought on board and this train will be sealed with two guards with machine guns at each door. They do not want your contagion to spread. So, like so many little Lenins in a sealed train, we shall speed across Europe. No-one will be allowed off until your home city is reached. I know that someone in this coach murdered my fellow countryman, Ladislav Mplmx, and I have until we arrive to find out who it was.'

CHAPTER ELEVEN

Where's Mr Dogdirt?

I settled back in my seat. Well, what a lot of
excitement! Murders, foreign policemen – still it
was nothing to do with me. I hadn't seen anything,
even though I'd been in the crowd when it
happened and, anyway, I had a travel book to write,
so I thought I'd better get on with it, otherwise
Methuen would take back the advance they'd given
me and I wanted to hang onto all those nice beads,
the mirrors and the clockwork mouse. I got out my
'Theroux' brand travel-writers' pen and my school
exercise book with all the useful information on the
back: the longest river in the world, the fastest
animal, the phone number of Amnesty International, how to cope with a drugs bust, how to
hot-wire a Ford Escort. How would I start my
travel book? Well, how about a nice bit of description – here goes then:

CHAPTER ONE

Chacun à Son Goat

Outside the train window the fertile North Italian countryside slid gracefully past, I could see field upon field of growing stuff. There was some wavy yellow stuff, some brownish stuff and some green stuff growing on trees. There were rockish-looking bits then some more growing stuff – the yellow stuff again, although it was different yellow stuff to the yellow stuff I'd seen before. Then on the horizon we passed a big thing. Then another different thing, different although just as high a thing: this was a big metal thing and was probably used for storing stuff in. Then the train passed some 14th century Renaissance courtyards, perhaps designed by Paul Veranazzi, although maybe they were post-war prefabs, I'm not sure.

The train picked up speed. There suddenly was a really interesting – no, it's gone. Here's a. . . ., shit, that's gone too. Into a tunnel – tum tee tum, diddle diddly doo dum doodle – out of the tunnel. The sky is full of starlings, or they could be bats or maybe Italian airforce planes, I'm not sure. In the distance men and women, or maybe trained barbary apes (I can't tell) are harvesting some more yellow stuff. Nearby a man is loading the yellow stuff into a truck. The truck is a Fiat OM75000 triple axle unit with a ZF 15 speed box with splitter driving the tandem bogie. The tyres are Michelin X85s.

Well, I think that's enough of that for a while. I think I'll go and show Zig-Zag my new trousers.

When I got to the guard's compartment at the very end of the train he was deep in conversation with the commie detective. I was just turning to go when the detective saw me.

'Fucking hell! Alexei Sayle! I don't believe it!' shouted Slobbo. 'I'm your biggest fan! Hello John got a new motor! Cak! Cak! Bloody cak, eh?'

I tried to speak but I couldn't get a word in.

Slobbo ploughed on, 'Listen I know it's a hassle but do you think you could just sign this for me, if you could just put it "To everyone in Detention and Brainwashing." Wow! They'll be really excited back home when they find out I met you. Go on, tell us a joke, go on, go on, do, do, do, tell us a joke, go on.'

When he shut up I didn't tell him a joke but instead expressed extreme surprise that anyone from a communist country in the Eastern bloc could possibly have heard of me.

'Are you kidding? We've seen all your programmes. *O.T.T.*, *Whoops Apocalypse*, *The Young Ones*, all great stuff. That Kevin Turvey he's great as well. Cor, I bet you all have a great laugh when you get together. Cor! My grandma loves you. Whenever you come on the telly she says, "I love that bloke – he's getting paid for shite. Taking all that money off them dick-heads for performing that rubbish!" I'll tell you one thing we love about you in my country is how you take the piss out of those miserable bastards, the Albanians. We all loved your Albanian World Cup Squad Song, but I don't think your record company ever really gets behind your records. . . .

THE ALBANIAN WORLD CUP SQUAD

THE ALBANIAN WORLD CUP SQUAD

A SIDE ALBANIA! ALBANIA! ALBANIA! (ALBANIXEY! ALBANIXEY!) MOXA 1
B SIDE ALBANIA! ALBANIA! ALBANIA! (COMMUNIST PARTY MIX)

The Official Song of the Albania World Cup Squad for 1982, especially composed by Albania's leading exponent of light music, ELYAS DROFFATS, and performed in its entirety by the lads themselves, all four of them.

THE SQUAD: 1. Johnnie (Guitar) BROXO 2. Rex (The dog he loves) 3. Mehmet OXO (Capt) 4. "Zippy" HENSHAW.

A THOUSAND YEARS OF ALBANIAN FOOTBALL...

 h! what a great delight would greet the student of history were he to turn his focus of attention upon the glorious history of Albanian history! Of what deeds of derring-do would he read! How his brain would reel in response to those tales of wonder! And if that same student were to naughtily digress in his study and examine other aspects of Albanian history, for example the recent miracle development bakelite reprocessing or the great leaps forward made in

that many of the fine porcelain fittings involved in these earth closets are of domestic manufacture. Unfortunately certain of the mechanical parts have had to be imported from North Korea creating a severe balance of payments deficit only partly offset by the miraculous 11% growth in Bakelite reprocessing.

But what has this to do with football! All play and no work make Istvan a dull comrade and nobody knows this better than Johnnie (Guitar) Smarties packet. Albanias

No. 4 shirt. Johnie lives quietly with his sister in Snoek province and enjoys nothing more than a quiet glass of goats curds. a good book and the occasional sexual liaison with an electric fence.

So what are Albania's chances in the 1982 World Cup?

"Golly gosh'" quipped Johnnie. "I don't know much about what we'll be capable of in the World Cup. but once I was sick in a vase."

SINGALONG BILINGUAL SONG SHEET

(A CUT-OUT-AND-THROW-AWAY SUPPLEMENT)

is not in it, hot breath.

Let us gaze back through the mists of time to the year 982 A.D. when, in Slobecq province, there lived a convent of nuns known by all and sundry as The Little Sisters of Self Immolation. Nearby to this convent was the Monastery of St. Everly. Each August 24th (The Festival of St. John the Baptist's Trousers) the Everly Brothers would cut off the head of an effigy of St. John and kick it through the gates of the convent and the nuns, of course, would attempt to kick it back. This sport attracted such attention from the people that it was soon necessary to build a grandstand, floodlighting and a system of computerised turnstiles that was the envy of the mediaeval world.

In modern times religion is severely proscribed by the people's court and religious ceremonies are illegal except in the back seats of motor cars at drive in movies. But football lives on. The present Director of Sport (Shehu Biryhani) is a fully fledged member of the Central Committee with wide ranging powers of arrest, search, detention, torture and death; a budget of almost 7,000 ratjabis per annum; and a muscular torso that is the envy of the Adriatic.

His brother Vimto is Director of Tourism and has worked himself almost to death in order to complete the full 5 year programme in the Hotel industry. Countless are the automatic earth closets he has personally installed and we are thankful

ALBANIAXEYLICH

Nostra voietsni josf andis amaxin teknikiolor,
drim, cok,
Nox centrovarfor jip jip bilhaley
Is voon nostra tris golskor mok mok,
Nostra stripkolor vox barf barf floorgaly,
Nox gardiin ezna wipp no septin heerrinx dis
bee o,
Ent si nifenfork si momenpop shimakest
Indesit enautomax in slapin rum furent
En granyild dox nox bulkenvorld dergratest

(CORUS)

Albanixey! Albanixey!
Represnov magrit tacher toree barf U.K.
Sanilav do jeysfluid den Espanay
Eniv no nostra cumup trums
Nox brijverk enamalgam agaplismin
Nox brijverk Wimpybar nos olga burgeration
Nox brijverk rampo vos flipflops
No kix durex Slobecqni
Vir dex blumin omshrokent
Wetdrim allin di globekni
Fab girstix rum furent
Hoopla! Rum furent Slobecqni
Hoopla! Rum furent Slobecqni
Moknot 23 Junex 1958 shoktrup
Hoopla! Rum furent Slobecqni

ENGLISH

We are the boys in turquoise, orange, pink and
green
Our centre forward runs like a comet
And if you disparage our goalscoring attempts,
The colour of our strip will make you vomit
Our goalie can't be beaten though he often
smells of fish
And his table manners scandalise his family
All our hotel rooms have modern plumbing
And our grain harvest is not nearly as bad as its
sometimes made out to be

(REFRAIN)

Albania! Albania!
Not nearly as repressive as Roumania
Easier to spell than Boueftsgwachgznia
And if we don't win any games
The secret police will confiscate our dentures
The secret police will take away our extra meat
ration
The secret police will shout at our slippers
We play for Slobecq province
Where the sweet omshroken blooms
We dream of her forests
And her modern hotel rooms
Oh! The hotel rooms of Slobecq
Oh! The hotel rooms of Slobecq
Sing along with me revolutionaries
Of the hotel rooms of Slobecq.

'Actually I've written some comedy stuff myself – I don't know if you're interested, just sketches and that. There's this one I've written about this political commissar and some black market vibrators. . . .'

'Shouldn't you be getting on with your investigation?' I said.

'Yes, I suppose you're right,' said Slobbo in a disappointed voice. He thought for a second, then brightened. 'But listen, you must stay. You could make a great routine out of this, 'cos there's some great laughs involved in police work – you know, amusing injuries, humorous points of corporate law. Please say you'll stay and get involved in this case with me, you could be like Dr Watson and I could be Disraeli and we could drop our trousers and . . . Go on. Say you'll stay. Pleeeeease, stay, go on, go on, pleeeease.'

'Oh, O.K.' I grudgingly agreed.

'Oh, great, great. Should I do a funny voice or anything? No? O.K. Well, to bring you up to date I'm just going through the files with Zig-Zag here getting a picture of the personnel on the train to locate the killer of Ladislav Mplmx.'

'I don't want to seem rude,' I said, 'But, as my grandma from the Old Country used to say to me, "Beware of Bulgarians carrying umbrellas". Isn't there a fair chance that your own people did him in?'

Slobbo mused for a moment. 'It is possible,

84

though not likely, I think. I have heard of no such plan and killing defectors is actually my department's job, so if there is an agent from another department of my government aboard I will want to find him and give him a good talking to. But enough of this talk – let's party. I have coca-cola and English cigarettes – let's have good fun and Tremeloes' records, then to sleep and in the morning me and Lex go hunting murderers.'

CHAPTER TWELVE

'Cor, That's a Big One' Said Reginald

The thing that makes rail travel superior to road for the observer is this – the roads go round the front. By this I mean that from the road the motorist sees the face that a place wants to project. All the billboards face the road, the Victorian columns and fancy doors face the street: the backs can fuck off. But that's where the train goes – round the back. From the train passengers see the backyards, the drains, the things they hide from the road–user. The only rail travellers who are exceptions to this rule happen to be the British Royal Family. The reason for their ignorance I will explain with a fairly true story:

A while back some people I know had their trees stolen. These people lived in a grim part of Liverpool, in a block of flats built between empty motorways which had been constructed for swarms of trucks that were only figments of the imaginations of corrupt councillors, guardians of the city who sold their city for silver tea services and holidays in the typhoid belts of North Africa.

However, the one thing you could say about the council was that they planted a fuck of a lot of trees. In fact, it sometimes seemed that they were trying to compensate for the loss of the Amazonian rainforest by re-creating it in Liverpool. Usually the trees planted were the wrong sort for the middle of a city, or they were plonked onto layers of toxic waste that had been dumped by bent firms owned by councillors and so the majority of them died. But outside these flats the trees, well, three of them, flourished. Not only that, but the council gave them A PATCH OF GRASS. People used to come for miles around to stare at the tall wavy things and the green stuff.

Then one morning the people in the flats woke up to find council workmen tearing up their trees and when the people asked why their trees were being stolen the council men said, 'Prince Charles is coming.' These trees were being dug up so they could be used to hide some blemish from His Highness, the Prince of Wales. They would be plonked down in some hole and left to die because it was felt that Prince Charles shouldn't see some decaying slum but should see instead wavy trees.

Well, when I heard about this I did some research and I found that the Royal Family – who travel by train a great deal – do not get to see what the rest of us see. All along the route of a royal train ride two-dimensional flats of industrious factories and pretty houses are erected to hide the burnt-out wrecks,

SCOTS HEROES

Lenny the Bruce

modern slums and rubble. Casting agencies provide healthy-looking, rosy-cheeked extras to wave and shout happily. The pasty-faced public in their paper clothes are kept well away. And that is why a train trip for the Royal Family is like a trip round Universal Studios, rather than the glimpses of the blown-out, carved-up heart of Britain that it is for the rest of us. So there.

CHAPTER THIRTEEN

David Bowie's Keyring

I partied till late with Slobbo and Zig-Zag then reeled back to my compartment.

During the night we were excreted out of Italy and trundled into Switzerland, a little rail-borne bundle of British filth and chaos, a broken arrow pointing towards England and the FUTURE. (That's what I call bloody writing, mate. I'm a certainty for a Booker or a Pulitzer if I go on at this rate.)

Just past Visp we clanked through a crack in the space-time continuum and went into the twenty-fifth century, but, as we were in Switzerland, nobody noticed. The only effect was that the price of a cup of coffee in the dining car went up to seven million pounds.

We came out of the other side of the time-warp with a bump which woke me up. I wondered for a few moments why Mr Brezhnev was standing over my bed holding a cup of tea and a Belgian bun, then I realised it was Slobbo bringing me my breakfast. He was as eager as a young crocodile to get on with the investigation and for me to make some sort of comedy routine out of it.

'Right, Lex,' said Slobbo. 'Now if we were conducting this investigation in my country I would just suggest to the subject that if maybe, oh crikey, he doesn't co-operate the secret police will happen to confiscate his sunglasses, then ho! ho!, lots of humorous terror, comic protestations of innocence. I pull some funny faces and do my comical voices and bingo! we have a confession and lots of material for you Lex, for your wacky T.V. shows. But on this train is more difficult. I have no secret police and cannot intimidate this lot, although I know a bit more about some of them than they might think. So I think we will interview some passengers at random to give the illusion that we know what we are doing, an old police tradition from around the world. First let us try – mmmmm "Mr Smith and Mr Smith" – that sounds phony enough. Come I have good English shoes and these shoes were made for walking, let's walk.'

As soon as I glimpsed them sprawling alone in their compartment I instantly and fearfully recognised them. I grabbed Slobbo and dragged him out of their sight. With a cold heart I realised we were in the presence of the infamous Moss Brothers, Sterling and Carl, at one time the terror of the London underworld, until their crimes caught up with them and they were sent down for ten long years.

In Dartmoor, at first, they were violent and

uncooperative, but after about a year they suddenly started attending various classes and rapidly turned into model prisoners and students. Sterling Moss finally obtained an external Ph.D. from Sussex University in Philosophy, Art History and the Politics of Real Ale. Carl had obtained his Ph.D. in Psychology, Social Studies and Applied Karate. Since their release there had been rumours that they had been using their enormous knowledge to commit crimes of a previously unheard of nature. There were tales of wallabies suddenly appearing in Trafalgar Square and seaside towns moving six inches to the left, but the Moss twins were never around and no-one else would talk.

Slobbo and I listened to their conversation while I filled him in on their identities.

STERLING: When I was in Wandsworf, on remand, right, this screw comes up to me and he's windin' me up, right. He says, right, he says, behaviourist methodology has been completely discredited by the structuralist stance on learning input.

CARL: Cunt!

STERLING: Bastard!

CARL: Causationalist!

STERLING: Right! So I says, right, 'If your causality is modular rather than thematic where does that leave your supposed methodology – you bollock-brained, prick-eared cunt?' Then I butted him in the froat. So he's staggering about

92

wif blood pouring from 'is nose muttering about De Bono's lateral thinkin' and he wasn't even lying down, when along comes these three other screws, right empiricists all of 'em and . . .

His voice trailed off as he noticed Slobbo and myself outside. For a second they went quiet then Sterling Moss, with a charming smile, invited us in.

STERLING: Slobbo, old chap, do come. We thought you'd be along to see us before long and we was interested in having a little chat about the socio-legal aspect of criminality in a socialist state.

Slobbo edged in. 'From your conversation your chats sound more like the Serbian–Bosnian war of 1847!' he barked with a silly smile on his face.

STERLING: Oh yes. Ha Ha. Very funny that, Slobbo. Oh and I see you have Mr Sayle with you. All Marxists together eh! Well, come and sit down both of you. Care for a little anchovy paste would you?

We sat down in their compartment and Slobbo began to question them.

SLOBBO: Well, first of all you do not seem like sports fans to me. Could you perhaps tell me what you are doing on this train?
STERLING: Well, we might ask *are* we on the train?

But I can see you are not interested in existential debates, so maybe I should pass that question to Carl to field.

CARL: Cheers Sterling. Well, it's a complex question you're asking Slobbo. If one says 'why?' one must also say 'what?', don't you think?

(*Crocodile enters stage left.*)

SLOBBO: Well you describe yourself on the train manifest as . . .

CARL: Businessmen.

SLOBBO: But you are in fact . . .

STERLING: Academics.

CARL: Of course we didn't used to be academics. We used to be . . .

STERLING: Community theatre co-ordinators.

CARL: You see it's like this: first we was criminals, real ones, as you probably know. But there's a problem with that . . .

STERLING: They put you in jail.

CARL: So we thought, we're bright, we'll get an education, then get involved in corporate crime, you know stuff like selling arms to both sides in small wars in the South Atlantic. Then you don't get bird, you get . . .

STERLING (*biting his hat*): A knighthood.

CARL: Exactly. But by the time we got out of chokey the old business game was getting a bit hard to get into, know what I mean? The real easy money was in 'the community'. There was real easy pickings in servicing 'the community'.

STERLING: You know, it's like famine relief for the distressed. No matter who the aid is supposed to go to, it always goes to the wrong people.

SLOBBO: And you are?

STERLING: The wrong people.

CARL: You see in the mid-seventies in many areas the government and local authorities had flattened cities. There was no shops, no pubs, no cinemas, nothing except blocks of flats and the people were growing crazy. So they thought they had better provide some entertainment for the poor working-class people, but it had to be entertainment that was GOOD FOR PEOPLE. Yes, there was plenty of easy money there for the wrong people. Community Theatre, Community Arts, Community Centres. Call yourself something like the Ring-Road Community Theatre Company, write some shitty community play like *We're All Potty – A light-hearted look at the history of Stoke* – then you go around housing estates in a Mercedes van frightening people and bellowing at little children through megaphones. We made thousands.

STERLING: But then wif the recession they gave up splurging money on disguising the awfulness of modern housing. All the easy money went over to disguising the awfulness of . . .

CARL: Unemployment. At first we thought we'd try to break into the legit theatre because seeing as that's a ruling-class pastime, it's safe from cuts.

But the mob is well established there – Peter 'Pretty Boy' Hall, Tom 'The Creep' Stoppard – so when the recession came along we got into . . .

STERLING: Further Education. See, the government is desperate to disguise the unemployment figures, right? And keep the kids off the streets. So if an enterprising academic with a sound knowledge of the workings of society and the political mind finds himself a college, bungs the principal a few quid, then mounts some course like 'Advanced Computer Studies for First-Year Urdu Speakers' or 'Nuclear Physics for Jamaican Steel Bands', he gets the money, splits it with the kids, they fuck off to carry on burning down the streets and you're home free with a great deal of loot.

SLOBBO: But surely you're not on this train as part of your academic pursuits?

(*A* SWISS BANKER *enters stage right and makes derisive gestures at his own leggings.*)

CARL: So true, chief, very true. The Further Education con is good money but it's not a big one. We reckon the big money's got to be at the point of greatest conflict.

SLOBBO: So you're on this train searching for . . .

STERLING: The total collapse of monopoly capitalism.

SLOBBO: On this football special? That's going a bit far, isn't it?

STERLING: Not really. Look at it this way; Britain

Exhibit A

NORMAN FALK
AND HIS SINGING SAUSAGES

was the first industrial manufacturing country in the world, right? Largest Empire and all that stuff. Now within the past ten years Britain has been losing its industry faster than an athlete chasing a sponsor. If it wasn't for the North Sea Oil money, we'd have the economy of Ethiopia. Our managers can't manage, our designers can't design, and our rulers can't rule. Over to you, Carl.

CARL: Cheers, Sterling. So what we have here is this. Britain is the first industrialised country to de-industrialise. Surely this is what must happen to all manufacturing countries eventually. But how will the next stage of development be brought about? There's no real sign of revolution in the conventional sense: the people of Britain aren't all marching about with red banners or buying dynamite and sitting in cellars calling each other comrade – there's none of that bollocks.

STERLING: But instead we find a deeper nihilistic violence. Wherever you go in Europe people are frightened of the British. Not just football fans either, but any Brits abroad are trouble. If you're in a restaurant in Vienna and there's some bastard with his underpants on his head being sick down your coat – you know he's British. As soon as they get abroad they all turn into little anarchists. So if you've got a trainload of British football fans traversing Europe there has to be conflict, a catalyst, a pointer to the future. And wherever there is conflict there is money to be made along the way, business to be done.

CARL: And sure enough, there has been conflict and business has been done. (GRUSHA *hides from the* SOLDIERS, *disguising herself as a chargehand/foreman in a light engineering works.*)

SLOBBO: So how do I know that you two didn't murder Ladislav Mplmx to promote conflict, for if I do not find his murderer there will be terrible trouble between Britain and my country.

STERLING: How can you say that, Slobbo? We are bystanders. We do not initiate but only observe, make sociological deductions and do a little business. Anyway we've got alibis.

SLOBBO: Alibis! How the hell can you have alibis? You were in the crowd when it happened.

STERLING: No we weren't. I was having sherry down the Vatican with a monsignor of my acquaintance. I just happen to have a polaroid photo of us together in front of a clock with me holding the day's paper. . . .

CARL: And I was in a sauna bath in Purfleet with the Chief Constable of Essex and several High Court judges. I just happen to have a signed affidavit to that effect which they gave me as a going away present. And if you want to know how I got back on the train so quickly, I employ a method of transport involving the transmission of molecules by radio waves, known only to myself and top scientists at Thorn E.M.I. Ltd. But when I have the time I travel by train 'cos it's nicer.

SLOBBO (*thinks for a while and then speaks*): Well, I think there is a certain seafood smell about your alibis but I am inclined to believe you were not involved in the murder, so I will leave you for now. C'mon Alexei, we have other people to interview.

The twins wished Slobbo goodbye in his own language, invited me to the launch party for a series of textile designs based on their prison experiences, and we left.

Slobbo was depressed. 'This is harder than I expected, Laudie Miss Claudie, and you can't make a T.V. or radio series out of this lot. And another thing. If they're twins why don't they look like one another. It's a mystery, as Toyah would say.'

Actually I didn't give a fuck about his problems anyway. I just wanted to get away and write my travel book, but this bozo kept dragging me round with him. I was just about to tell him to bugger off when a dreadful squealing and squarking gave evidence that Zig-Zag was back on the air.

'Squeal, Squark, Squelch. Good after Christmas general. How are the Csar's hamsters? Well, have I got some news for you! Mystery upon mystery piles up around this train, boys and girls, welding torch, tangerine, bicycle. I have just heard from off the B.B.C. World Service News that the star of our own dear team, Jimmy 'Boy' Wonder has disappeared and in fact has not been seen since he was sent off twenty minutes before the end of the game – along with the murdered Ladislav Mpmlx!'

(An audible gasp ran through the train.)

'We will bring you updates on that story as and when, banana, bandana, mañana, Nicaragua, squeeze. Meanwhile, here on the train that socialist sleuth, Slobbo Arsich, continues his investigations and he has roped in Alexei Sayle to be his Boswell or perhaps his Sancho Panza or maybe his Little Chef, who knows? If you were listening earlier you will have heard Slobbo come in and macaroon, select eight records he would take with him to the Gulag Archipelago. Okay, great, we've got some exciting things coming up for you later. Martin from compartment six will be talking about his hobbies, which include talking to fish and being head of the British Council and he will be taking calls on irritating newsagents. I'd also like to remind everyone that there's a film crew aboard and if they ever resolve their dispute they could be popping into your compartment anytime, roasting you with hot lights, pointing whacking great cameras at you and telling you to just act natural. Anyway, automatic fan belts, here's a record specially for Police Captain Slobbo Arsich who'll be round later to check your alibis and it's Robert Palmer and *Looking for Clues*.'

In an afternoon heat haze we waved a cheerio to

Switzerland and re-entered France. Outside the window I could see peasants practising their gallic shrugs and boating on wine lakes. The stores of food on the train were starting to run dangerously low and there was a near riot, but fortunately somebody remembered that at Macon there was a huge store of three-course English dinners circa 1941, including brown windsor soup, braised steak and boiled potatoes and college pudding with custard.

These meals had been dropped by parachute to the bemused French Resistance by R.A.F. bombers. I saw the handiwork of my uncle Reg in this. You see my family's war record was not particularly glorious, in fact my cousin Hector avoided the call-up by spending the war hiding out in his brother's aircraft carrier. The only hero was my uncle Reg. At the start of the war Reg was a student at the Sorbonne doing HND Catering and Hotel Management. He was a well known figure in the smart circles of Paris and knew all the great French personalities of the time: Sartre, Camus, Genet, Tintin and Snowy, Astérix. When the war came he joined the Resistance and was in charge of catering and stores liaison with the R.A.F. He arranged for the drop of many useless and pointless items such as tins of Swarfega and two hundred-weight bags of nutty slack, before the exasperated French turned him over to the Gestapo.

The train was halted on an embankment and

French riot troops, openly sneering at our cuisine, threw the tins of braised beef up towards the clutching hands which strained from every window of the train.

It was late afternoon but the sun, which had beaten down on us all day long, was still making itself felt. The stench from the other coaches was almost overpowering. I decided to go for a lie-down in my compartment. Lance, of course, was in there and wanted to hear some stories about all my show-biz friends but I told him I just wanted a lie-down 'cos my nerves were bad 'cos of the dog and that shut him up. I'd just got settled when bloody Slobbo came barging in saying we had lots more people to interview. Honestly, that man is a nuisance.

This time we had to go and talk to Kimberley Clarke – Miss T.V. Failure 1976. I didn't want to be seen talking to her, well it's not good in my business to be seen mixing with pathetic failures, love – that's why I stay away from Kenny Everett.

And to add insult to injury when we got to her compartment the disputing film crew had formed a picket line over the doorway and as I went in some Trotskyist Assistant Cameraman's Assistant shouted: 'I see you crossing the picket line, Sayle! You sell-out bastard!' What a bloody cheek – me a sell-out. I've never sold out in my life, honest comrades!

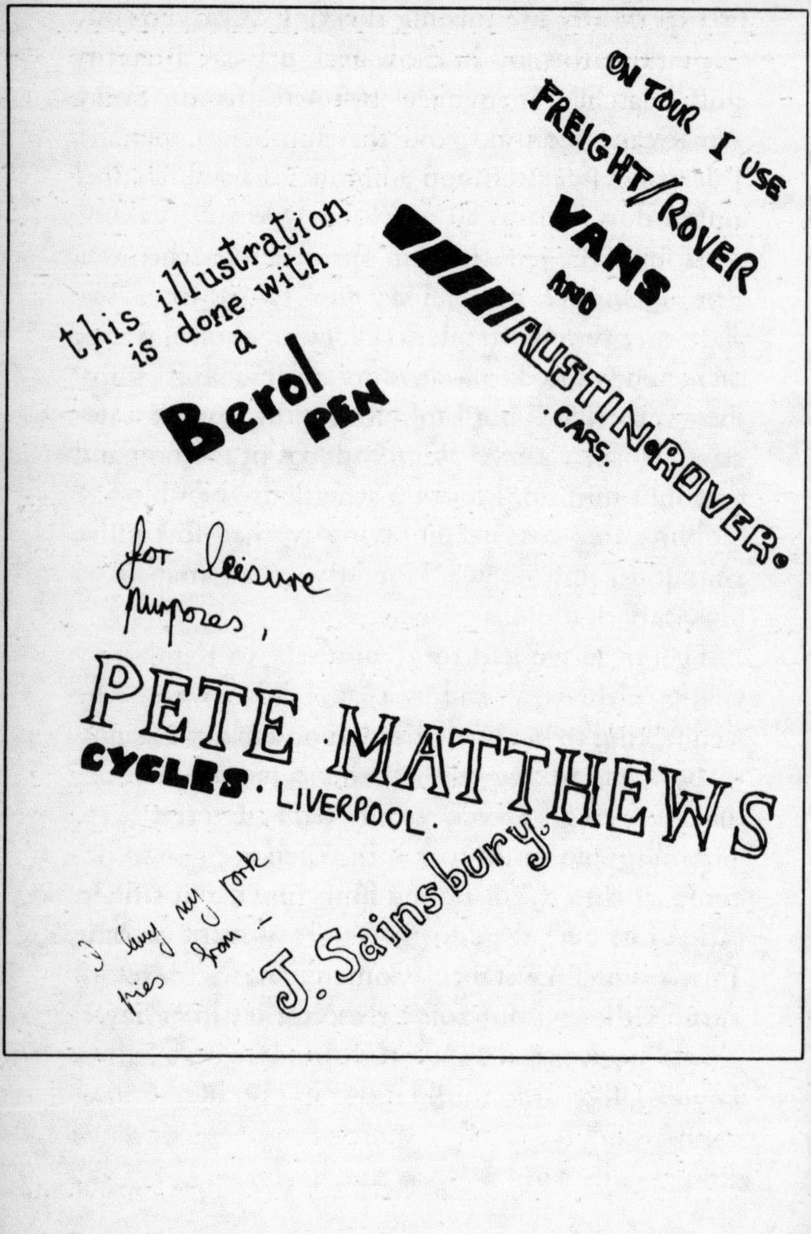
ON TOUR I USE
FREIGHT/ROVER
VANS
AND
AUSTIN ROVER
.CARS.
this illustration
is done with
a
Berol PEN
for leisure
purposes,
PETE MATTHEWS
CYCLES · LIVERPOOL ·
I buy my pork
pies from -
J. Sainsbury.

I spend my life turning down T.V. adverts and invitations to play in show-biz sponsored charity golf matches against celebrity teams of South American dictators. And the number of benefits I've done! I can tell you comrades, I have not sold out.

Slobbo barged straight into the compartment and sat down on somebody from Wardrobe, who didn't seem to mind too much. I just stood and tried to act the cynical observer by curling my lip in a rather nice way I have. Kimberley Clarke was staring out of the window and ignored our entrance. Slobbo however was not to be put off.

'Miss Clarke I would like to ask you a few questions, please.'

Kimberley did not answer.

'Miss Clarke.'

She turned to Slobbo and with extraordinary venom shouted, 'Oh why don't you fork awf?'

Now it's a funny thing about posh people, they can be anything they want. If they want to be photographers and they're the Queen's cousin, it's fixed. If they want to be hippy-junkies, it's fixed. They can be heads of the Secret Service or have their own crazy satirical comedy shows on television. Although, for some reason, they very rarely choose to work on the production line at British Leyland. The only things they can't do are swear or dance. They can't say a short proletarian 'fuck', it always comes out as 'fork' and if you see them at a dance 'having a bop' at some May Ball or something, it always looks like a room full of windmills, all flailing away shouting 'Fork awf you old baaastaaard' at each other and slinging buns about. I hate the bastards. I wonder why that is?

Slobbo was not to be put off.

'Miss Clarke, I have been talking to some of the people on this coach and you were seen in the murder crowd with a stills camera. I need to know if you took photos of the murder perhaps? Did you know something was going to happen? I need to know the truth.'

Kimberley: 'I told you and your fat friend to fork off and I meant it, you pair of caarnts, and anyway what does a commie like you know about the forking truth? Hawk, hawk, hawk.' She laughed and her laughter rang through the train. And it was as if one was in all the places of power where that laughter continually rang: the BBC, the Stock Exchange, the Ministry of Defence. And one thought that puts one in one's fucking place.

Slobbo was stung into replying: 'More than you think.'

Kimberley: 'Oh bawllawks! Your press is censored. Anybody who deviates from the government line is locked up. Hawk, hawk.'

Slobbo: 'Oh pardon my irony, but in your country the public is fed an undiluted diet of truth – Ha! As we say in my country "show me a pickled egg and I'll show you an after-dinner snack".'

Kimberley: 'What does that mean?'

Slobbo: 'Absolutely fuck all. But that is my point. I have seen your English papers and your "free" English television – "Sexy Susan's naughty nightie really sets the profs boiling down at the Imperial Institute of Social Anthropology where she is a research fellow. Now it's over to Bob for an item about a talking tree." I know you Western journalists, you make up the story before you meet whoever you're supposed to interview. Your papers are full of fiction but your public thinks it is all true. At least in my country everyone knows it is all lies. I mean all the news readers wear army uniforms. Every time we read about new triumph in State Pram Factory or great leaps forward in Bauxite reprocessing we have a good old laugh, but at least we don't believe any bollocks about Iron Ladies and talking trees.'

Kimberley: 'I don't know what the fork you're talking about.'

Slobbo sighed: 'Of course you don't, but at least now you are talking to me so now maybe answer some questions please, yes?'

'No. Fork off!' said Kimberley.

I thought it was about time I took a hand in this interrogation, I tried the old hard and soft technique. Slobbo had been relatively nice, so I thought I'd be the baddy.

'Fucking answer the man or I'll fucking kill you,' I screamed – I get a bit carried away sometimes.

Kimberley looked at me for a minute then said: 'Oh piss awf! You working-class fool.' And her aristocratic eyes looked down her aristocratic nose at us, as if we were two Portuguese au pairs who had done something unforgivable with the soufflé.

I was annoyed then.

'Listen mate,' I said, 'It was a well-known fact in media circles that you used to be the girlfriend of Jimmy Wonder. "How I tamed Jimmy Wonder" stories in the Sunday papers until he gave you the push last year. But maybe you wanted to get back in with him by killing Ladislav Mpmlx because he got Jimmy sent off or something like that. And I also notice that you don't seem too bothered about the fact that you're not getting any filming done. Have you decided to retire or are you onto a different story of some kind? Ha, ha. Answer me that then.'

Kimberley: 'I told you – I'm not answering any of your forking questions. Now fork awf.'

'Nice weather for the time of year,' said Slobbo.

'Oh fuck it, let's go,' I said. 'C'mon Slobbo let's leave her for now. Let her sauté.'

And we left.

CHAPTER FOURTEEN

1846: Repeal of the Corn Laws; Lord Tomkinson's Bending-Down Act; Repeal of the Dick Tax; Introduction of Stephenson's Offset Spitting Machine

That evening I was assailed with doubts. Should I be helping with this investigation? Should I get on with my book? Is Charlie Chaplin really funny? Is Snoopy? Do you have doubts? I doubt if they're as good as my doubts.

The fact that I got free rail travel when I was a youth nearly made me deeply unfashionable. When I was about fifteen or so hitch-hiking was the groovy way to get about – but I never fancied it, being a railway child. But unfortunately I was sharing a house with some really hot-shot hitch-hikers like the legendary 'Mitch the Hitch'. Mitch would never walk anywhere. He would just stand at the end of the path from the house with a sign that just said **SHOPS**

And some of the others were hippy hitch-hikers – they'd stand at the start of the motorway with a sign that said

FAR OUT

So we'd be sitting in the house and somebody'd shout, 'Let's hitch to Leicester' and we'd all rush off, but I'd make some excuse, sneak away from the rest, get the bus into town and then get the train to Leicester, for nothing. But of course I'd get there before anybody else so I used to invent stories about how I got there so quickly, like, 'Well, I was in this pub car-park and this helicopter lands and the pilot says excuse me, chief, do you know the way to Leicester and I said I'm going that way I'll show you!' Or I'd say, 'Yeah I got a lift off a bloke in a Lotus who just happened to be delivering a kidney to somebody in Leicester.'

Now, nobody believed these stories, but, being hippies, they'd believe any pseudo-mystical shit that anybody wanted to tell them, so this rumour started to go round that I had the power of teleportation and that I in fact travelled down ley lines to Leicester. And that is why I always get served first in wine bars.

I'm not getting very far with my book. I know what I'll do – I'll do one of those witty, weird cartoon books that people only buy at Christmas and keep in the lav.

"IT'S A PIECE OF PISS," SAID ABDUL.
"ALL YOU DO IS DRAW SOMETHING STUPID
AND IT GETS PRINTED
IN THE OBSERVER COLOUR SUPPLEMENT".

or

MARCUS WAS CHARGING
HIS BATTERIES

Yes, I might try a few more of these.

As the train rattled through the dark European night, leaving behind Chartres, Versailles, Paris, unnoticed, the passengers started organising ways of passing the time. In one compartment there was aerobic dance, in another creative cookery. One group of fans were putting on an entirely new interpretation of Peter Brook's *The Ik* to rapturous reviews and full coaches. One coach had declared war on another and were demanding access rights to its Polish corridor. People were dancing, drinking, making love, stuffing paper up their noses and squawking like chickens – all the things that people do to pass the time on trains.

In our luggage van there was yet another football quiz, but as the contestants could only come from within our sealed coach, there was no competition for 'The Brain of Football.' Pretty soon everybody got fed up with the quiz, then somebody said, 'Hey, let's have a party.' And it was just like all the parties I've ever been to. Somebody printed mimsy invitations: 'Mish and Tish invite you to their bash. Bring some plonk but don't honk.' And Chris is there of course, looking all moody, then Judith turns up with this guy Terry who's the liaison officer for the Youth Training Scheme project she works on and Chris goes all crazy and locks himself in the bathroom (the one Mish is going to turn into a dark-room when she gets it together) and threatens to kill himself by drinking a whole bottle of Head and Shoulders and then starts crying. And

Judith goes up to take care of him and stick her fingers down his throat and Terry gets all jealous and starts dancing with the Deputy Head's wife. Then a group of top houseplant psychologists turn up from Guildford with a stock of old Beach Boys' singles . . .

Ralph ALWAYS TRIED TO MOVE WITH THE TIMES

. . . and things really start hotting up. Somebody makes punch with absolutely everything in it and everybody drinks lots and gets squiffy.

The floor was throbbing with flabby information retrieval officers, the sweat dribbling off their stringy moustaches, wobbling their amply filled Marks and Sparks safari trousers, completely out of time with Barbarbarbarbarbarbarbara Anne, trying to chat up equally sweaty radiographers in low-cut crushed velveteen fishermen's smocks by telling them about this fabulous holiday they had on the Adriatic island of Domestos and how often they go jogging and how they used to have a Morgan and saying 'This is a late parrot' and 'Plectrum, Under-manager' and 'Hello John got a new motor' and pissing themselves laughing as if it were funny or something. Then somebody says, 'Hey everybody, there's some Stones records here.' Then suddenly everything went red and I tried to chase everybody out with a meat cleaver but a couple of fans pinned me down and I can't remember anything for a bit. . . .

When I came to they'd left me slumped in a corner, the party was still going on, but quieter now. Near me Slobbo was talking to 'The Brain of Football.' I listened.

Slobbo: 'By golly! You know a lot about football.'

This seemed pretty obvious to me but it seemed to please the Brain.

'Why thank you very much,' said the Brain.

It was funny but when he was answering questions on sport his voice was clear and deep, but

Philip HAD JUST POPPED OUT TO STRETCH HIS LEGS

when he spoke in conversation he had one of those nutter's voices that you hear coming from the man in the laundrette with the alarm clocks in the pocket of his raincoat who keeps telling you about dolphins.

He continued: 'Oh yes, I know more than anybody about football. When I'm in a quiz I always get the answer right. Always. Always. It's very very important to me.' And there was a strange light in his eyes.

'And this particular team, of course,' said Slobbo.

The Brain of Football got more heated and a beatific smile spread over his face.

'Oh, the lads. Yes I know every conceivable fact about the team – total weight in kilograms, aggregate shoe size. I've got all their records and everything. And, if I might say so, I am also a personal friend to the team. When they did the "League Champions in Dub" album at Compass Point in Nassau I was there. I helped out at the re-mix at the Powerhouse in New York. Oh they all know me and I run errands for them, clean their cars and all that. Of course when they get transferred I won't talk to them. Why, Jimmy "Boy" Wonder treats me just like an uncle. I used to help him run the team's Drama and Debating Society. We did *Faust*, *The Merchant of Venice*. You know if Jimmy hadn't been a footballer he was such a bad actor he could have been with the National Theatre.'

Slobbo: 'I know where you're coming from. I have to be very close to my team. I keep a record of who they see. I have to protect them from people like you.'

The B.O.F. was confused: 'I don't protect them from people.'

Slobbo: 'No, what I'm saying is I protect them from people like you. In fact on the morning of the match you visited Ladislav Mplmx at the team hotel and gave him a parcel. You were seen by one of my informants in the team. Why did you do that? Were you on an errand for somebody in the team perhaps?'

B.O.F.: 'I don't know what you're talking about!'

Slobbo: 'Well, I cannot force you to answer me. If we were in my country I could send the secret police round to confiscate your goldfish, but here . . . Oh well. Be aware I know you visited the murdered man. I will put the pieces together before the end of this journey. Cheerio for now.'

I was being sick near a big packing case with writing on it. Slobbo saw me, helped me up, took me into the corridor and propped me against the wall. I was in that post-drunk self-pitying mood you can get into.

'Oh Slobbo, my mate, my dear old pal,' I cried. 'We're not getting very far are we? We're useless, useless. We'll be back in the City by tomorrow evening and everybody will disperse and you'll be deported and we'll never ever find the murderer. Oh Slobbo, what'll we do?' Then I started crying and was sick again, all over Slobbo's brogues.

'Hello, remember me, Gavin? You know, the one who's playing the tremendously exciting role of the dead body of Ladislav Mplmx? Well, the author himself has just been sick all over my packing crate – that's exciting isn't it? That's worth five years rigorous training, studying to play fictional characters, isn't it? I know it's a hard business but I think I've been in it long enough, I've had several major successes in fringe books, and I expect more out of life than playing a dead person in a book of dubious sales value, and having the author throw up all over me.

'You know I've just thought of something. If I'm the dead person Ladislav Mplmx, then I must know who killed me. Let me think. What happened just before? I snuck into the crowd, I hung about a bit, then everybody started running and somebody come behind me and . . . of course. That's who did it!'

'O.K. Mr Fatty Sayle. I've got a message for you. If you don't want me to give away the ending by revealing who did the murder, then I suggest you give me the part of a new character in the book with lots of exciting attributes or I'll tell the readers who killed me. O.K. You've got five seconds, ready? One . . . two . . . three . . . right, it was. . . .'

CHAPTER FIFTEEN

Well, That's a Turn-up

Mr Saunders, the exciting new character, strode down the corridor, his blue eyes twinkling under his thatch of blonde hair. His long stride covered the ground with athletic ease, his enormous penis nestled in his custom-made underpants, by Quadratti of Paris. He felt happy and at one with the world. He was well respected and powerful and was sure he was going to be able to take a major part in this murder investigation. Approaching him down the corridor was a stocky figure in a ripped mohair suit with an evil face, topped by a skinhead crop. Mr Saunders seemed vaguely to recognise him.

The figure smiled broadly as he came up to Mr Saunders, then swiftly pulled a pin out of a round green object which he stuffed down Mr Saunders' Pierre Cardin pullover. He then opened the centre door of the coach and pushed Mr Saunders out of it. As he tumbled through the night air Mr Saunders thought, 'You bastard. You fucking fat. . . .' The round object in his jumper gave a small click and right after that Mr Saunders exploded into a thousand non-speaking parts.

CHAPTER SIXTEEN

I Should Coco

As I closed the door I heard a muffled crump, receding down the line, behind the train. It was too early to go to bed. I'm always full of nervous energy after one of my red mist attacks, so I went for a walk up and down the coach a few times to practice my aerobic walking exercises. I bopped past my own compartment where Lance sat upright on his bunk, fast asleep, dreaming of cheese and chutney sandwiches. I skipped past the closed and shuttered door of Rabbi Feinstein's compartment. I minced past the picket line outside Kimberley Clarke's compartment. I fancied an argument, but when I looked in she didn't seem to be in her compartment, so I bounced on past the compartment of the Moss twins, Sterling and Carl. I stopped for a minute and listened to their conversation.

'So the woman in the cakeshop says do you have any empirical evidence that that is a pork pie and not, for instance, a cement mixer. Then she twatted me on the head with the cash register.'

'I had a similar experience at the Museum of Modern Art. I was studying the Jackson Pollocks when this bloke. . . .'

I tap-danced backwards the rest of the way to the front of our coach. By the door the same fans who had been so impressed by Rome's incomparable old buildings, were standing looking out into France and chatting.

'Hey look at that bar – it's still open and it's way past closing time.'

'Maybe they've got a special extension from a magistrate 'cos they've got a function on or something.'

'Or maybe all the people in there know the manager and they've got a stay-behind or something.'

'It's fucking difficult to get a drink outside licensing hours in England.'

'Oh, I don't know. It's not too bad if you live anywhere near Smithfield Market in London – the pubs open early in the morning for the meat porters, so you can usually get a drink in a boozer if you remember to keep a pork chop on your head.'

'Or if you're beyond territorial waters – the bars on oil rigs are open until 11.30 and they sell duty-free fish.'

After a while I got fed up with this intellectual discussion and skipped back to Zig-Zag's bolt-hole at the back of the train. I found him sharing a late-night glass of plum brandy and a Kit-Kat with Slobbo. The last thing I wanted to do was to go on investigating but Slobbo was still convinced that I could wring some humour out of us getting insulted by potential witnesses. Slobbo saw me as I attempted to slide off imitating a bit of furniture.

'Ah, Alexei!' he said, 'There you are! I have decided it is time now to interview this Rabbi Feinstein. I'm sure you'll find some wacky funny Jewish humour in what he has to say and,' turning to Zig-Zag, 'I have had a thought. I believe you have radio-telephone contact with England?'

Zig-Zag: 'That's right, your holiness, cocoa, balaclava.'

'Well, in that case, I want you to get in touch with somebody from the supporters' club back home. We found a return ticket for this train journey on the body of Ladislav Mplmx. I reckon that as all tickets were bought through the supporters' club there may perhaps be some record of who bought them. It's a slim chance, but we might as well give it a try. Now come on, Alexei, let's go and talk to the reclusive Rabbi Feinstein.'

Back down the corridor we went. Slobbo stopped and hammered on the sliding door of the Rabbi's sleeper compartment. No reply. Slobbo knocked again and tried the handle – the door was locked and there was still no answer. Slobbo knocked once again and then, scowling, started to head–butt the door at four second intervals. Finally a voice with the most ridiculous 'Chewish' accent I have ever heard called out from inside the locked cabin:

'Vot iss it? Who is nockink outzide mein dwoor?'

Slobbo shouted: 'This is Captain Slobbo Arsich. I am investigating the murder of my fellow country-man Ladislav Mplmx. Please let me in. All I want is to ask you a few itsy-bitsy questions.'

The Rabbi didn't seem to want us to come in. He was positively insistent.

'No! No!' he screamed. 'No you cannot cum in tonight, for tonight iss der holy Chewish feast of Flanaka and it iss written that on zat night a man must zit in zolitude wiss a pound of turkey giblets behind each ear and zum bratwurst in each shoe and he must hide himzelf from ze eyes of uzzer men!'

'That's a bit bloody convenient,' said Slobbo, in a whisper. Then he resumed shouting: 'Come on, be a sport and let us in, there's a good chap,' he wheedled.

But Feinstein wasn't to be persuaded: '*Nein! Nein!* For zis iz ze holy veek of Shamlaluh ven all Rabbis are beholden by Gott to be zircumspect about zeir movements or ass it iz written in ze holy book – ze *Shnadach*, ze prophet Bongo vill descend wiss her head of molten paper clips and ze Israeli airforce will bomb your civilian suburbs. Eh-ayee, eh-ayee!'

'Oh, for fuck's sake, just let us in, you old bastard!' shouted Slobbo.

'Ay-eeh! Ay-eeh! Benzol! Benzol! It iss forbid-den, for it iss written on ze feast of Shambulah, and the intervening days of Protozoa a man must hide himself from ze light, sustained only by cream-crackers and lemonade pop and he must balance retail produce on his head to ze value off forty sheckels minus V.A.T.! It iss zo written. Ay-eeh! Ay-eeh! Benzol! Benzol!'

'Oh, all right. Shut up, we're going,' yelled Slobbo. 'Come on, Alexei, we're wasting our time here. But I must say it's a bloody useful thing, religion.'

And he stormed off back to Zig-Zag's cabin in a fine old Slavonic temper.

There was nothing more that could be usefully done that night. The next day would be the last opportunity to track down the murderer of Ladis-lav Mpmlx. So far we had received no remotely relevant information from anyone and we had no suspects. Also I had no book. According to the B.B.C. World Service, Jimmy 'Boy' Wonder still hadn't been found and we had no clues. We would surely need our wits about us on the morrow.

Cry 'What ho! Sir Hal,'
Lest between the scringly shinhank
And cut loose the cut-purses and scallywags!

Shakespeare, I thought, there's something important there, something about the *Merchant of Venice*, but I drifted off before I could figure out what it was.

CHAPTER SEVENTEEN

Surplus Value

During the night we again crossed the English Channel and morning found us chugging through the neat rolling green stuff of Southern England.

I woke up feeling depressed. I had done hardly any work on my book and we would be back in the North by this evening and everybody would be dispersed. I thought I might as well get some exercise, so I jogged down the carriage. As I hopped past Zig-Zag's compartment I saw that he was on the radio-phone. I went in, waved a good morning to Slobbo and listened.

Zig-Zag put the phone down. 'Morning Lex! Mr Mugabeeee, off the lane motoring certainly. Well, Slobbo, we've come up with something very puzzling this time. That was the supporters' club on the phone. I gave them the serial number of the ticket for this train which we found on the body of Ladislav Mplmx, they checked their files and that ticket was part of a batch that were given to the team players to give to their girlfriends or whatever. That particular ticket was given to, cocoooo, bananas, it was given to – Jimmy "Boy" Wonder!'

For a moment there was a perplexed silence between us. Then Slobbo banged his fist on the wall.

'Jimmy Wonder! What bloody help is that, seeing as wherever he is, he's missing. He's not on this train. He can hardly be suspect. Oh, what are we going to do? If I don't find the killer before we arrive the secret police will defoliate my allotment.'

It looked as if Slobbo could go on in this vein for quite some time, but he was stopped by the sight of Kimberley Clarke going past. This wouldn't have been that unusual except she went past on the outside of the train.

Zig-Zag acted like lightning. While Slobbo and I were rooted to the spot Zig-Zag shot out of the door, zig-zagged across the floor, shot back in, jumped on the seat twice and finally slammed on the emergency brake.

The train shuddered to a halt in a shower of sparks and curses. Slobbo, Zig-Zag and myself jumped down from the train. A few fans tried to get off as well, but the soldiers from the international peace-keeping force (who haven't been mentioned much) levelled their weapons at them – it was a stand-off. I shouted at the soldiers to keep the fans aboard at all costs and we raced back down the track with Slobbo carrying Zig-Zag for greater speed. Out of breath and panting we reached Kimberley

Clarke — her body lay sprawled across the track. I applied the accepted medical test for brain death — I showed her a copy of the *Daily Star* and she laughed at the cartoons. She was dead all right. In her hand she clutched a cartwheel hat with dreadlock-like ringlets stuck to it. 'Rabbi Feinstein!' breathed Slobbo.

We turned back towards the train just as a blackcoated figure tussled briefly with a soldier. They fell on the ground and the figure grabbed the soldier's sub-machine gun, then leapt athletically across the tracks and disappeared into the railside undergrowth. Slobbo grabbed Zig-Zag:

'Make sure that the train does not move and keep everyone aboard until we get back. C'mon Alexei — let's get him.'

We ran down the line to the train. From his coat Slobbo pulled a huge .45 calibre service revolver. I shouted to one of the guards who threw me his Sterling 9mm machine pistol. Then we crashed off into the undergrowth in pursuit of Rabbi Feinstein, or whoever he was.

Together Slobbo and I ran through fields of growing yellow stuff; the Rabbi's path was marked by trampled crops. Now, I'm no naturalist but after a while I noticed there was something wrong with the vegetation we were running through. I pulled up a stalk of yellow stuff and studied it as we ran. It had a strange artificial look and weird texture, the colour was too bright and clear. Looking at the end of the stalk I saw it had writing round the bottom, like a stick of rock, all the way through it. It said 'ASTRO-CORN, 100% Polyester corntype growing thing.' We darted through a recently made hole in the hedge which bordered the field. On the hedge was a small label. It said 'Pozi Privet – the premier name in acrylic hedgerows. Ask to see our range of fibreglass wild–life.'

When we scrambled our way onto the road it all started to make sense. A large sign at the edge of the highway told us in bright modern letters:

Milton Springsteen! The showpiece New Town of Britain. You saw the posters everywhere:

Towards the town, down the main road which was called 'The Dave Clarke Highway Number Five' we saw a black-coated figure running like hell.

Slobbo shouted, 'There he goes,' and pelted off. We sprinted down the road, which after a minute ended in a large empty car park. Signs and barriers told us that the only highways through the centre of Milton Springsteen were architect-designed cycle-ways and bikes were provided free for our use. In the distance a cloud of dust and gravel told us that our Rabbi, or whoever it was, had already taken advantage of this offer. Slobbo and I followed suit and grabbed a couple of rusty bikes. The choice was limited to either those little folding shopping jobs made out of old gas pipes in Poland or those big green Raleighs that they equip community policemen with. We mounted two of the latter, I slammed the Sturmey-Archers into second and leant on the cranks. Grit flew. I popped a wheelie and flew in the direction of town. Pretty soon I was gaining on the Rabbi while Slobbo floundered in my wake. In the corners of my vision on the edge of the cycle track, I saw unfinished houses, fields of cracked mud and dead trees flip past.

There were very few people about. Some sat disconsolately outside the shells of buildings with notices written in chalk saying 'Fire Station' or 'Law Courts'. When they saw us screaming past they would jump up and shout in weedy voices 'It's quite nice really!' I bent low over my handlebars, trying desperately to decrease wind resistance while my legs pumped madly. We hit a dead straight stretch and I flipped the Sturmeys into top. Ahead of me the Rabbi did the same. Though I was gaining inches on him, he was surely some kind of athlete to keep this kind of speed up.

Like three little whirlwinds we reached a particular edge of town, which happened to be Milton Springsteen's officially designated Chinatown. Of course no real Chinese people had been stupid or desperate enough to move there, so instead English people were wandering about dressed up in Chinese clothes and pigtails. When they saw us they shouted, 'It's quite nice leally!'

As the Rabbi turned a corner, Slobbo squeezed off a shot from his service cannon. It missed the Rabbi but hit a building which exploded as if it were cardboard, which, as the bits floated past us, it in fact turned out to be. It appeared that there was considerably less to Milton Springsteen than met the eye.

I banged the gears down into second, slid one-footed round the corner, switched the Sterling to single shot and whacked one off. My shot blew apart some mechanical sparrows which had been tastefully grouped on a church roof. Awwk! they shouted as Slobbo and I pedalled through a blizzard of springs, coils, wire and artificial beaks. The Rabbi turned in the saddle and let off a burst of 9mms from his Sterling. They whistled past us, ripped apart a rubber tree and an android yokel who was in the middle of saying, 'Milton Springsteen. It's quite nice. . . .' BANG 'Awghah really Springsteen nice awk!'

Slobbo squeezed off another .45 which blew apart the Rabbi's back wheel. As the bike dis-integrated beneath him, the Rabbi did a forward roll over the handle-bars and was running before his feet hit the ground.

I slammed on my brakes. Slobbo drew up behind me. He was impressed:

'He's a bit fucking athletic for a Rabbi, if you ask me. They're not normally known for their gym-nastic abilities.'

Before we could stop him the Rabbi had sprinted into the main branch of Habitat which was situated behind a dried up fountain in the central shopping piazza. Abandoning our bikes, we chased in after him. I caught a glimpse of a black coat and immediately fired. Ceramic, plastic and metal sprang apart as I blew away a whole shelf full of those tasteful pastel ceramic table lamps that you see fucking everywhere. It came to me in a flash that I was achieving one of my life's ambitions – to shoot up a major branch of Habitat. With a wild cry, I switched the Sterling to rapid fire and pumped half a magazine into a row of Cotswold couches – the air was filled with a mixture of foam and chipboard.

'Take that you bastards,' I screamed.

For a moment I was filled with an overpowering desire to destroy this entire shrine to pre-packed mediocre 'good taste', but a shot from the Rabbi, which narrowly missed me and destroyed some pottery things for growing cress in, brought me back to the business in hand. The Rabbi was holed up near the lighting department. Slobbo and I began a pincer movement to trap him. I dodged through Linens, Wallcoverings and Roller Blinds, while Slobbo circled through Furniture, Crockery and Ready-Made Lifestyles and Philosophies.

I was just crawling past the latest in the Pleatex range of paper blinds when up popped the Rabbi, gun in hand. I was paralysed by his face – a face known to me through a thousand endorsements, charity walks and post-match interviews. He was raising his sub-machine gun to the firing position when a shell from Slobbo's .45 caught him in the chest blowing him sideways. He was dead before he hit the floor. When I could finally speak I said, 'That was not a Rabbi.'

'No,' said Slobbo.

'That was,' I said.

'Jimmy "Boy" Wonder,' said Slobbo. That was when the plate glass window caved in.

Back at the train the multi-national peace-keeping force had had their work cut out keeping the people in our coach – murder suspects all of them – aboard the train. The rest of the fans, cooped up for six days as they had been, made a break for it across the fields of Astro-corn towards Milton Springsteen, which lay like a washing-up bowl full of Portuguese crockery on the horizon. Their temper, for a raging mob, had been on the jovial side of berserk until they had looted an off-licence in a fairly gentlemanly manner and found that all the bottles were filled with coloured water. Then they went completely ape-shit. By the time they came crashing through the window of Habitat the whole town was ablaze.

The fans intent on further damaging Habitat took a short while to notice our little group over by the Pleatex blinds. When we finally registered on the mob – me, Slobbo and the body of Jimmy 'Boy' Wonder – silence spread through the smouldering store. All faces stared towards us, cold, hard, slowly calculating what to do next. Slobbo took charge of the situation. He rose with the corpse of the football star in his arms.

'Explanations will be given, back at the train,' he said and with that he moved off through the crowd, gingerly stepping over shards of provençal crockery. A few of the hard lads from some of the other coaches, looked like they might jump Slobbo, but I poked the ugly, ventilated snout of my Sterling at them and they backed off, muttering threats about what they would do if explanations were not forthcoming, about how Slobbo had just happened to blow away their favourite football player in the whole world.

We trooped back through fields of waving nylon. Behind us we left the burning cardboard buildings and the wonky clockwork birds, gradually being covered in a pall of acrid black smoke. Across the fields drifted a final, feeble, 'It's quite nice re . . click'.

We mounted the embankment and reached the train. Slobbo climbed the steps of our coach. Around him the peace-keeping force, dusty and battered, formed a protective ring. Slobbo addressed the crowd around him.

'Fellow sports fans! All your questions will be answered. I now know who killed my countryman and why. It will be explained to you in a way that is both entertaining and instructive. We will have one final grand football quiz. It will be broadcast throughout the train and the whole story will be told. Now return to your carriages – the train will re-start in five minutes.'

CHAPTER EIGHTEEN

Too–rye–aye

T!.e last of the fans had been hustled and crammed back onto the train. The emergency brakes had been taken off. Our journey re-started and the great football quiz began. Zig-Zag had appointed himself the compère of the quiz and had adopted the style of a T.V. game-show host. He told a few racist gags, introduced his lovely hostess for the evening then . . .

Zig-Zag: 'Good evening, ladies and gentlemen, dinner gong, Fleetwood Mac, thank youoooo. Welcome to the football quiz of quizzes. It's a lovely evening here in Rugby, just outside Rugby, in the countryside quite a way from Rugby, oh fuck it. The quizmaster for this evening is that great socialist detective Mr Slobbo Arsich. First prize is a life sentence in a prison of your choice, second prize is a night on the town with Red Rum. The contestants are all the passengers on this last coach of (in big letters)

THE TRAIN TO HELL.

every one of them a suspect in the murder of Mr Ladislav Mplmx, socialist footballer from the land of Slobbo Arsich, balloon bollocks. Amongst those appearing are the Moss Twins, Sterling and Carl, two of Britain's least wanted men. We also have the distinction of having two dead people on our panel – a big hand please for the lifeless corpses of Rabbi Feinstein, or should I say the late star of our own dear team Mr Jimmy "Boy" Wonder, and our second corpse – Miss Kimberley Clarke! Who can tell what contribution they might have to make! Moving along now we have Lance, the little man with the big imagination and next to him the man who always gets the questions right – The Brain of Football. Also, of course, we have with us Mr Alexei Sayle, smutty comedian and author – what part will he play in this exciting dénouement? Plus everybody else from our coach – the film crew, the fans who stand by the door and a lot of other unnamed extras. Now here is your celebrity guest quiz-master for the evening, as we get nearer and nearer our own dear town and time gets shorter and shorter in a desperate final bid for the truth – Mr Slobbo Arsich!'

Slobbo sat behind a desk facing the contestants, his quiz cards in his hand. He looked serious.

'Right, first question,' he said. The first question concerned the existential contradictions within the concept of the sliding tackle. 'The Brain' was in there immediately, quoting from Sartre to support his thesis.★ The second question Slobbo asked was whether a dog could play for the England National Squad. This was a bit too simple for 'The Brain' and Sterling Moss gave the correct answer which was, of course, that the dog could play 'but only if it was deaf, blind and crippled'. The Brain's face screwed itself into a twisted map of anger and frustration at losing even a single point in a football quiz.

Question three was on the singing centre-halves of Silesia – a famous footballing miracle when a

★'L'homme qui s'appelle Nobby Stiles, ou également Chopper Harris (Chelsea et Brentford F.C.), quand ils commettent le tackle sliding, affirment l'existence du choice libre de toute l'humanité.' Jean-Paul Sartre (Paris St Germain et Tranmere Rovers F.C.), *L'Existence et Le Football*, Éditions Foulard et Fatbastard, Paris, 1979, 30 francs.

group of ethereal heavenly mid-field players appeared to a Portuguese peasant girl and revealed to her the West German squad's game plan. The Brain of Football answered with frantic speed and beamed at everyone round him when told he was right.

Question four was a bit of a strange one. Staring straight ahead, Slobbo asked in a monotone, 'Can any of you tell me which player in my country's team was known by the security forces, including myself, to be a homosexual?'

Everybody looked blank at this one. Slobbo spoke again, 'I must point out that this is a valid football question and if anybody fails to answer then that shows a gross lack of football knowledge.'

There was still bemused silence, until a rattling sound drew attention to the Brain of Football who was shaking on his chair, a thin hissing escaped from his lips. He was trying to choke down words which nevertheless erupted like vomit.

'LADISLAV MPLMX!'

he screamed.

Slobbo remained stony calm. 'Very good,' he said, 'two points. Now for a follow-up question: Name the homosexual on your own team.'

There was a roar of denial from the fans, but through the noise everyone heard the Brain shout,

'JIMMY WONDER!'

'Right again,' said Slobbo. 'For part three of this four-parter, who killed Ladislav Mplmx?'

Now there was silence all round. The Brain, sweat streaking down his face, seemed for a moment to hold the words down, but the compulsion to answer was too great. 'I killed him,' he said in a whisper.

Slobbo now relaxed, simply asked, 'Why?'

Slowly it came out from the Brain, told to us all in his nutter's voice: 'Well, you must have figured it out by now but I suppose you want everybody to know. Well I guess it doesn't make any difference now. It all started when the two teams – yours and ours – met for the first time. I'd known Jimmy from when he was an apprentice with the club. He was always one of my favourites and he'd always seemed to be quite a one for the ladies. He used to tell me some of the tricks he got up to – man's talk, you know, between sportsmen. . . . Anyway, after that first match Jimmy and that Ladislav met and . . . well, I don't want to go into it but he told me they just fell in love. At the time Jimmy was carrying on with Kimberley Clarke, but he gave her the push when the team got back to England. She wasn't pleased at all. She thought Jimmy would help her get her career going again. While they were apart Jimmy and Ladislav kept in touch through letters and phone calls that Ladislav made when he was in the West – playing matches. When they found out that the teams were going to meet again they worked out this plan that would allow Ladislav to defect actually during the match. That's when Jimmy got in touch with his old pal and confidant, the Brain of Football. He thought I'd be pleased to know he was in love, even if it was with another bloke! Anyway I said I'd help him with his stupid plan. When we got to Rome I was to get to Jimmy's boyfriend and give him the team regalia to disguise himself and also a ticket on this train which Jimmy had got off his free allocation. Ladislav would use that ticket to get past the guards and ticket collectors and onto the train where he would hide in the compartment which Jimmy had booked in the name of Rabbi Feinstein. He thought he was some kind of master of disguise because he'd played Shylock once in the team's end of season production of *The Merchant of Venice*. Jimmy would then board the train dressed as the Rabbi – they'd be together the whole way back to England. The other thing was that Jimmy had got me to get in touch with that stupid bird – Kimberley Clarke. While they were on the train she would film interviews with them and they'd give her the whole story, their affair and everything. At first she thought the strike would put the mockers on the filming, but she showed me how to use the video camera one night. It was easy really, and she took still photographs of Ladislav in the crowd, when he was trying to board the train. It would have been a big scoop for her, made her a top T.V. person again.

Jimmy and Ladislav also arranged that they would foul each other during the game so they'd both get sent off and so Ladislav could make his escape. And it all went like clockwork, until I killed him, of course.'

It had gone very quiet in the luggage van. The only sound was the snickety-snick of wheels.

'And why exactly did you kill him?' breathed Slobbo, the quizmaster.

'Everybody would have known that we had a pouf on the team. I wasn't going to let that happen.'

Slobbo: 'I find this difficult to believe. You killed somebody just to prevent some imagined minor disgrace to the football team you happen to support?'

The Brain spoke and it was odd but his Nutty Norman voice had gone, 'Not the team, you fucking fool – the City. Look out there, we're arriving now.'

And indeed we were. We looked out the window and there across the river was the City.

B.O.F.: 'Look, Slobbo, look at it. Miles and miles of fucking rubble, ninety-nine per cent unemployment, the rest of the country would like to put a wall round this city – except for the team that is. The only pride we have.

'Now it's all right to be a pouf in the Arts or the Theatre or some nancy game like tennis – but not football, mate. That's the people's game, a man's game, mate. No bumboys allowed. Can you imagine the stick the lads would get from the opposing fans – they'd never survive it. The team would die and the City wouldn't be far behind. I told Jimmy that Kimberley Clarke had killed his boyfriend because she was so upset at him chucking her for a man. I thought he'd finish her off seeing as she was the only other one who was in on it. I didn't think the stupid pouf would get himself killed as well. Still, serves him right, silly queer bastard. Anyhow the team's saved and the City, and I don't regret what I did for football and my home team. That's why I killed Ladislav Mplmx – civic pride. I expect they'll offer me the Freedom of the City. I bet all the real fans here agree with me. Now they know what I did they'll all want to be my mate. Isn't that true, lads? Eh, lads?'

He beamed round at the assembled supporters' club. They stared back, thoughtful looks on their faces as if they were buying a new car and couldn't decide on what upholstery to have. One of them spoke, 'You're a fucking nutter,' he said. 'It's only a fucking game, after all.'

The fans nearest the exit began to shuffle out, heads down as if their team had just been beaten at home by a third division club. The Brain grabbed at the sleeves of the departing people, pleading with them. Finally one of them turned, 'The best thing you could do, mate,' he said, 'is die.'

Soon the only people left in the luggage van were myself, Slobbo and the Brain. Slobbo reached up and pulled the communication cord. The train stopped. Slobbo slid the carriage door open, a parcel of cold night air breathed into the stuffy luggage van. The Brain stood all alone by the open door. The few orange street lamps that still worked twinkled on the hill behind him. Our train hung in mid-air, halted on the big bridge over the brown river.

CHAPTER NINETEEN

Bending Up

I didn't see Slobbo the next day. He had a certain amount of explaining to do, about shooting Jimmy Wonder for instance, so it wasn't until the day after (his last day in England) that I saw him. I met him at his hotel, it was early in the day and he was feeling frisky. We went outside and before I could stop him he dragged me into one of the hundreds of cruising beat-up taxis and shouted to the driver 'Show me the sights!' The driver took us to an M.F.I. carpet warehouse and the swimming baths.

We paid the cab off and strolled through the centre of town, past rows of boarded-up shops and boarded-up people, rubble, dirt and chaos. Slobbo had never seen anything like it. 'When our capital was destroyed by the Germans we rebuilt every bit of it exactly as it was. But you people you have pulled down all the buildings. You have no past left, you have destroyed it. O.K. I know you British had things to be ashamed of, child labour, imperialism, colonialism, Max Bygraves . . . but there was no need to destroy your cities. Now I see how a football team could be so important.'

We walked on through the rubble. 'It was nice of him to throw himself off the bridge,' I said.

'Yes,' he said. 'Neat. And you know he had a point, the football world is certainly centuries behind the rest of society – it would have done the team a lot of harm. But now the story won't get out. Now the killer's dead there won't be any police action and all the fans will certainly keep quiet. Rumours will spread but the truth will never be known.'

'Of course the only way it could be told,' he continued, 'would be if there was somebody on the train who knew all the facts and had to write something like a book really fast or his arse would be in the wringer. So he'd write it all up and have it published.

'But he'd have to be a real shit to do that, wouldn't he?'

Mandarin Humour Classics

Charles Addams
ADDAMS AND EVIL

H.M. Bateman
THE MAN WHO . . .

Alan Bennett, Peter Cook, Jonathan Miller &
Dudley Moore
THE COMPLETE BEYOND THE FRINGE

G.K. Chesterton
COLLECTED NONSENSE AND LIGHT VERSE

Peter Cook & Dudley Moore
DUD AND PETE: THE DAGENHAM DIALOGUES

Noël Coward
THE LYRICS OF NOËL COWARD
A WITHERED NOSEGAY

Harry Graham
WHEN GRANDMAMA FELL OFF THE BOAT

A.P. Herbert
UNCOMMON LAW
MORE UNCOMMON LAW

Jerome K. Jerome
THREE MEN IN AN OMNIBUS

Edward Lear
THE NONSENSE VERSE OF EDWARD LEAR

Tom Lehrer
TOO MANY SONGS BY TOM LEHRER
WITH NOT ENOUGH DRAWINGS BY RONALD SEARLE

Ogden Nash
CANDY IS DANDY

S.J. Perelman
THE MOST OF S.J. PERELMAN

R.E. Raspe
THE ADVENTURES OF BARON MUNCHAUSEN

W.C. Sellar and R.J. Yeatman
1066 AND ALL THAT
AND NOW ALL THIS

James Thurber
LET YOUR MIND ALONE!
THE MIDDLE-AGED MAN ON THE FLYING TRAPEZE
MY WORLD AND WELCOME TO IT
COLLECTING HIMSELF
FABLES FOR OUR TIME
FURTHER FABLES FOR OUR TIME

Also available in Mandarin Paperbacks

Steve Bell
THE IF . . . CHRONICLES
IF . . . ONLY AGAIN
ANOTHER LOAD OF IF . . .
THE UNREPEATABLE IF . . .
IF . . . BOUNCES BACK
IF . . . BREEZES IN
THE VENGEANCE OF IF . . .
THE REVOLUTIONARY IF . . .
MAGGIE'S FARM: THE LAST ROUND-UP

Simon Bond
101 USES OF A DEAD CAT
101 MORE USES OF A DEAD CAT
UNSPEAKABLE ACTS
ODD VISIONS AND BIZARRE SIGHTS
SUCCESS AND HOW TO BE ONE
TEDDY
UNIFORMITY
STROKED THROUGH THE COVERS
TOTALLY U.S.
ODD DOGS
HOLY UNACCEPTABLE

Sandra Boynton
CHOCOLATE
DON'T LET THE TURKEYS GET YOU DOWN
CHRISTMASTIME

Claire Bretecher
FRUSTRATION
MORE FRUSTRATION
MOTHERS
STILL MORE FRUSTRATION
WHERE'S MY BABY NOW?

Mel Calman
BUT IT'S MY TURN TO LEAVE YOU
HOW ABOUT A LITTLE QUARREL BEFORE BED?
IT'S ONLY YOU THAT'S INCOMPATIBLE

Chris Garratt and Mick Kid
FILE UNDER BIFF
FAXES FROM BIFF

Caroline Holden
DANGER, GOD WORKING OVERHEAD

Barry Humphries and Nicholas Garland
THE COMPLETE BARRY MCKENZIE

B Kliban
CAT
NEVER EAT ANYTHING BIGGER THAN YOUR HEAD
TINY FOOTPRINTS
TWO GUYS FOOLING AROUND WITH THE MOON
WHACK YOUR PORCUPINE

Yolanda Nave
WELCOME TO OUR COMPANY

Alexei Sayle and Oscar Zarate
GEOFFREY AND THE TUBE TRAIN AND THE
FAT COMEDIAN
GREAT BUS JOURNEYS OF THE WORLD

Posy Simmonds
MRS WEBER'S DIARY
PURE POSY

Norman Thelwell